MW00651656

Conch Republic

Vol. II

Errol Flynn's Treasure

Look for other Western & Adventure novels by
Eric H. Heisner

Along to Presidio

West to Bravo

Seven Fingers a' Brazos

T. H. Elkman

Mexico Sky

Short Western Tales: Friend of the Devil

Wings of the Pirate

Africa Tusk

Cicada

Conch Republic, Island Stepping with Hemingway

Follow book releases and film productions at:
www.leandogproductions.com

Conch Republic

Vol. II

Errol Flynn's Treasure

Eric H. Heisner

Illustrations by Emily Jean Mitchell

Visit our website at
www.leandogproductions.com

Illustrations by: Emily Jean Mitchell
Contact: mlemitche@gmail.com
Website: www.mlemitchellart.com

Dustcover jacket design: Dreamscape Cover Designs

Edited by: Story Perfect Editing Services – Tim Haughian

Hardcover ISBN: 978-1-7353257-4-3

Printed in the United States of America

Dedication

The Muse:
Whoever they may be…

Special Thanks

Amber Word Heisner, Emily Jean Mitchell,
Chris Tidwell, Billie Beach, Jr.
& Papa Filip

Note from Author

Where a fiction writer comes up with story ideas is often a very different place from where they write. I spent a vacation holiday at Ian Fleming's former residence in Jamaica - Goldeneye. I don't think I'll be writing any 007 spy novels, or be establishing a tropical island as my official writing retreat, but a friend casually mentioned, "Oh... is this location going to be in your next book?"

Jamaica wasn't on the idea board at the time, but after another visit to Key West for the Hemingway Days festival, this story manifested itself and had to come out. I thought, what better place for a fictional writer to travel than to the island where a spy-novelist dreamed up a classic character, who was an international playboy, and who in actual life rubbed elbows with the real deal during his time on the island – Errol Flynn (actor, writer, sailor & treasure hunter).

Enjoy another unintentional adventure of the mystery-adventure writer who went to Key West to make a life.

Eric H. Heisner

June 20, 2020

I

It is just another bright, sunny day on the island of Key West. Birds call out loudly to the new morning and insects chatter all around. The sound of a garden leaf blower, humming in the distance, is followed by the droning sound of a city street-sweeper machine approaching.

On an avenue, off the main gathering street of Duval, an unassuming historic house sits on a large estate of lush, green gardens. Tall shade trees cover the grounds, and the sprinklers kick on to put a rainbow mist over the stone walkway. Behind the residence sits a carriage house garage with a wrought iron stairway leading to an apartment above.

The amplified clicking of an old-fashioned typewriter drifts out through the open window of the garage apartment. The tapping on a keyboard clatters away at a steady staccato. Seated at a fancy-carved table that serves as a writing desk, the mystery and adventure novelist, Jonathan Tyler Springer – alias "J. T. Springs", sits before a modern laptop computer. His fingers move at a steady pace like a pianist at the keys.

After a moment, it becomes apparent that the keyboard sound is a digitally reproduced effect of a vintage typing machine

Following the blink of the cursor, Jon's gaze moves steadily across the screen. His lips move slightly, mouthing along with the words written. The loud, electronic tapping of typewriter keys continues as he writes, and he remains oblivious to the quaint, apartment around him.

Above a wooden bookshelf, an African trophy mount hangs on the wall extending over shelves loaded with collectable hardbacks and a Royal Quiet de Luxe typewriter. The entirety of the garage apartment seems to be outfitted in classic 1930's Hemingway island-style, complete with rattan furniture and an old, leather club chair.

The steady tap of fingers on the keyboard comes to a stop, and Jon glances up from the lighted screen of the laptop. He clicks off the volume key, muting the mimicked clicking sounds of the vintage typewriter. His gaze travels over to an antiquated rotary telephone on a side table and then to the clock display at the bottom corner of his computer screen.

Seemingly satisfied with his writing progress for the moment, Jon clicks the save icon and pushes back in the creaking desk chair. He stands and stretches his shoulders, as he looks down at the text-filled computer screen and smiles. "Time for a little jog…"

The screened door of the apartment opens and closes with a groan of the hinges and a slamming bang as Jon exits. Dressed in a t-shirt, shorts and running shoes, he descends the metal, spiral staircase and trots along the damp garden path toward the front gate.

Swinging the decorative, wrought iron entry gate open, Jon steps into the street and almost immediately bumps into a gentleman with a trim, grey beard and dressed in khaki attire. The sudden appearance of the older gentleman startles Jon, and he steps back to apologize for nearly plowing over the distinguished-looking figure. "Uh, sorry… Excuse me, sir."

The white-haired gentleman offers a friendly wave, steps aside, and continues on his way while Jon gapes, flummoxed, as if he might possibly recognize and know him. He stares a moment, watching the backside of the departing gentleman wearing the out of place, adventure-safari outfit. Shaking off the odd encounter, Jon bends over to stretch, grabbing for his toes, and then he bounds down the sidewalk on his usual running path.

~*~

Trotting along the streets of Key West, Jon passes the shops lining Duval Street, as the business owners clean the sidewalks in front of their stores and prepare to open for the day. Traveling south, jogging over a block and to the west, Jon passes a tall masonry wall that appears to be made from a random mix of salvaged bricks and mortar. He slows to a stop at the front of the secluded house and jogs in place a minute, as he glances to the wood sign near the walled entrance.

Ernest Hemingway
~ Home ~
Open 9 a.m. ~ 5 p.m. daily

Peering around the brick wall to the Hemingway Home Museum, Jon looks through the closed gate at the yellow house with green storm-shutters and well-manicured gardens. He watches a six-toed cat bound across the lawn and then leap to the front porch and curl up for a nap in the sunshine. After stretching again, Jon continues his jog. At the end of the street, he jumps the curb by the colorful, red-tipped marker of the "southernmost point" and proceeds to the beaches beyond.

Jon pauses to look over the crushed-coral shoreline, which was imported to make up the sandy beach of Key West. He stares out to the water with its multiple tiers of green and aqua-blue colors and enjoys the sunlight of the new day on the horizon. His ear catches the rumbling of a marine motor approaching in the distance and, after a short while, a sport-fishing boat with a lineup of four outboard motors rounds the end of the island and powers up, cruising toward open water.

Jon breaks his idling gaze from the wake of the boat, looks down the stretch of uncrowded beach and continues on his jogging path to complete his morning routine.

~*~

At the bottom of the spiral staircase leading up to the garage apartment, Jon does several cool-down stretches. He pauses when he hears the sharp, bell-ringing tone of the vintage telephone coming from inside the carriage house. Hurrying up the winding stairway, Jon swings open the creaking screen door and lunges inside. Eagerly, he swoops in to grab the telephone handle from the cradle and puts the receiver to his ear. "Hello…? Hello?"

The only answer, from the other end of the phone line, is the monotonous dial tone of a disconnected and missed call. Jon swings the coiled receiver cord over the telephone base and hangs up the handset. He gazes around the tidy, sunlit apartment, until his attention finally comes to pause on the coffee table where an envelope, addressed with fancy handwriting and a foreign postmark, rests.

Jon takes a seat on the padded arm of the club chair and reaches over to grab up the old telephone receiver again. Using the rotary dial, his finger spins a series of numbers, while he reads a scrap of folded paper from the nearby table. The sound of the dialed numbers winding through the rotary device finally gives way to the ringing-tone of the placed call.

Jon sits and waits, while the old telephone continues to ring again and again and again without anyone answering. "Come on, Rollie… Pick up…"

After another few rings, Jon hangs up the telephone, looks to the fancy envelope and back at his laptop monitor. He reaches over to the writing table, closes the folding screen of his computer and stands to peel off his sweaty t-shirt. Tossing the damp shirt over the back of the chair at the table, Jon mumbles aloud to himself, "Guess I'll have to find him at the Conch Republic Tavern."

II

In a cluster of mangroves off the island coastline of Key West, a pieced-together floating shack sits perched on an assemblage of empty oil drums. The empty barrels are attached together with a deck over the top to make a resourceful, shanty home. A dinghy sits tied-off to one corner, and the whole domicile is decorated with scraps of "found treasures" ranging from broken lifesaving floatation rings to lobster traps and random items of shipwreck salvage.

The narrow deck surrounding the floating cabin is lined with an assortment of discarded boat bumpers in dingy and faded discolor from white and orange to sea-grass green. Inside one of the shuttered windows, the sound of a footlocker being dragged across the wood-plank floor is heard followed by the scraping rattle of a key in an old lock.

The rusted click of the locking mechanism opens up and gives way to the clunking release of the hasp on the trunk. Slender, sun-tanned fingers with oversized joints and pugilist knuckles ceremoniously open the tattered lid. Inside the trunk is a red, silky fighter's robe that is moved aside to reveal stacks of curled photographs and a pair of vintage-leather boxing mitts. One of the photos on top of the stack is of a lean, dark-skinned youth standing shirtless next to a heavy-set man sporting a dark moustache, a smile and short-cropped haircut.

The gnarled fingers reach into the truck and lift the top photograph from the mixed odds and ends. In the lower left-hand corner of the photo, an ink-scribbled inscription reads: *To a sparring partner & friend - E. Hemingway*

~*~

Freshly showered, with his hair combed back and outfitted in a short-sleeved button-down, Jon steps out from the garden gate from where he resides. He proceeds to walk down the empty sidewalk toward the main thoroughfare of Old Town, Key West. After a short jaunt along Duval Street, Jon notices the main drag seems a little busier than normal at this hour. He turns onto a side street, glances at the throngs of gawking tourists gathered on the boulevard and murmurs to himself, "Hmm… There must be a cruise ship that just came in and unloaded for the day."

Jon continues away from the crowds for another block. Before reaching the street corner, he turns into a beer garden under the shade of a giant banyan tree. Stepping up to the out-of-the-way drinking establishment, Jon gazes at the faded signage over the door that reads: *Conch Republic Tavern*.

Entering the dimly-lit barroom, Jon proceeds past the brass plaque on the wall that relates the history of the saloon as one of Earnest Hemingway's primary carousing locations. He steps up to the unusually crowded bar and looks around, searching for a familiar face. Instead of finding the bartender, Jon gazes down the bar-top at a lineup of old, white-bearded gentlemen, all dressed in tan-khaki hunting or fishing attire. He looks up to the painted portrait of Hemingway over the bar and back at the assemblage of look-alike gentlemen. Blinking his eyes at the unusual sight, Jon steps back from the bar and gazes around the room.

Nearly half the occupants in the establishment appear to be outfitted as Ernest Hemingway. In utter amazement, Jon pushes up against the counter again and leans forward on the bar-top. The female saloon owner, Angie Storm, walks over to him and reaches out to put a friendly hand on his shoulder. "How're ya doin' there, Jon?"

He turns to her, gazes at the familiar-looking faces and puts on a perplexed smile. "I think I need a drink."

Angie laughs sweetly, grabs up a clean pint glass and turns to the beer tappers. "You want the usual? Sunset ale?"

Jon leans across the bar-top, and talks to her just loud enough to be heard over the din of the crowded barroom, "Uh... Is there something going on in town that I'm missing?"

She finishes the draft pour of beer and places it before Jon. "The Papas are filling up the town for Hemingway Days. Happens every year around Ernie's birthday weekend."

Jon swallows a sip of the beer and takes a gander around the room again. "Gosh, I thought it was some sort of a *Safari Santa* convention. Why do they do it?"

"Mostly to raise money for charity, but they are a good group of guys and have a lot of fun around town."

Jon grins, as he takes another look down the bar at the Papas and their hands filled with beers and cocktail glasses. "Drinking for charity...?"

"There is a good bit of that fun, along with a fishing tournament, arm wrestling match and running of the bulls."

With surprise, Jon turns toward Angie. "Did you say, running of the bulls?"

She grins while commencing to fill a customer's drink. "Not as dangerous as you might think, unless someone gets heat stroke or drinks too much and trips on the curb."

The idea of dozens of Hemingway-looking characters in the tavern starts to grow on Jon, as he takes another sip from his beer. "There is always something going on."

Behind the bar, Angie slings one drink across the slab and looks over her shoulder at Jon as she prepares another. "Yep. How's that writing going?"

He nods his head with a smile. "It's coming along."

She turns to set the drink on the bar-top and winks. "Slow and steady finishes the race. Hold on… Be right back." Angie pats him on the arm before she moves down the bar to deliver the cocktail. Jon leans back on the bar rail and gazes around the room. Music plays just above the chatter and the multitude of Hemingway look-alikes appear to be having a good time.

Angie swipes a white towel across a spill on the wet bar-top and comes back to where Jon leans back on the rail. "So, what's the deal with you getting down to Jamaica?"

Jon takes another swallow from his beer and replies, "Last I heard from Rollie was that one of the engines was torn apart for an overhaul, and it would be down for a week."

Angie nods and watches the bearded occupants of the room. "Yeah… Ace mentioned that last night when he was in. Said he and Sandy should have it put together in a few days, but Rollie probably won't be able to get away anytime soon, what with having to catch up on customers."

Jon turns his head and pivots around to face Angie. "It's fine. I'll just have to send a message to my friend in Jamaica and explain my situation."

"It's a shame to pass up on an invite for adventure." She smiles and winks teasingly at Jon. "You could talk to Carlos about using his boat to get you down there."

Getting a bit of a cold-sweat at the mention of Carlos, Jon shakes his head and closes his eyes. "You're kidding me? It was only a week ago that he ditched me on a rubber raft in the middle of the Gulf Stream.

She laughs her charming bartender chuckle and grins. "Yeah, when traveling beyond Cuba, he's probably not your most reliable option."

Taking another gulp of his beer, Jon thinks aloud. "Maybe I'll just get a job washing dishes on a cruise ship heading in that direction."

"Or, you could stow away as a handsome traveling companion for some rich, old lady looking for someone to play a hand of cards with."

He laughs at her suggestion and replies, "Maybe she'll want to play strip poker?"

Angie lifts an eyebrow and raises her chin to the side. "You'll be lucky if that's all she wants to play…"

Jon grimaces, and then he seems to have a thought of his own. "You know, that isn't the worst idea…"

"It's not a good one either."

Jon takes the finishing gulp of his drink and sets down the empty beer glass. "Not that she owes me any favors, but maybe I could contact Jeaneé Reneé?"

Angie tilts her head inquisitively at the mention of the affluent, landowner and part-time Florida Keys resident. "Yeah, she probably knows a bunch of lonely, old ladies."

"No, no… Not for that." He crinkles his brow at the bar owner and gives her a frown. "I was thinking, maybe she has some other sort of connections that might get me to Jamaica?"

Mystified, Angie shrugs and looks over to another white-bearded customer in need of her bartending services. "Good luck getting in touch with her, but it's worth a try."

He gives a tap of his fingertips on the bar slab and gives Angie a departing wave. "Thanks. See ya later, Angie."

She returns the gesture with a casual salute and warm smile. "Good luck, Springer."

III

Walking down the main tourist thoroughfare, Jon notices the amount of tourist activity is even busier than it was earlier. Spotting several Hemingway-looking gentlemen, he smiles to himself and then cuts through the crowds on the sidewalk. The shrill trumpeting sounds of Spanish bullfighting music suddenly thunders through a loudspeaker at a nearby bar, prompting a loud celebratory cheer.

~*~

Back at his current place of residence, Jon enters the gated yard and trots along the path through tended gardens. He makes his way around the main house to the carriage house apartment behind. He climbs the old, spiral stairway, swings open the screened door with a creaking rattle and is startled by an unexpected voice coming from inside.

"Well, hello there *J. T. Springs…*"

Jon stands backlit in the apartment doorway and lets his eyes adjust to the dimmer light of the room's interior.

His jaw drops open as he exclaims, "Holy smokes! Treadwill, how'd you ever find me?"

With a month's growth of beard, seated on the rattan sofa is Jon's pal, and Navy SEAL operative, Chaz Treadwill. The career military man sits forward on the couch cushion, grins widely and offers a habitual salute to his old friend. "Merely a serendipitous coincidence, pal. I just returned from an overseas deployment and ended up in Miami." He touches the whiskers under his chin and continues. "Putting a call in to your cell phone got me an odd conversation with a pleasant lady from Michigan who was more than happy to brag about meeting you in Key West."

Jon steps into the apartment and makes his way over to take a seat in the club chair opposite the sofa. "Dang, if you're here to rescue me, I could have used your help last week."

"Yeah? It's better late than never." Chaz smirks as he looks Jon over. "You don't look too much worse for wear. What happened?"

"Scott Fulton was in town."

Chaz grunts and widens his eyes understandingly. "Sorry I missed him this time around. I was on international business in the Middle East, unfortunately." The Navy SEAL looks around the well-decorated apartment and lets his gaze linger on the writing table with the closed laptop computer. "Are you getting any good writing done?"

"Some."

"Where is the next adventure off to?"

Jon reclines back in the soft leather chair and exhales. "No more pulp-adventure stories for me. This new one I'm working on will put me in league with other serious writers out there and earn me some respect."

Chaz drops his smile and looks very disappointed. "Ah, too bad. I really enjoy your adventure stories."

Jon shrugs his shoulders and glances to his computer. "Well, the serious writing thing isn't going that great anyway, and I'm flat broke after Fulton's social call."

The visitor seated on the couch flashes a charming grin. "So, we might not have heard the last from J. T. Springs?"

"My California literary agent sure as hell hopes not." Jon stands and walks over to the small apartment kitchen. Stepping over a military-style gear bag tossed on the floor by the doorway, he glances back at his Special Forces friend. "You just got off a mission?" He opens the fridge and peers in. "You want something to drink?"

"Sure… Whatever the Conchs are drinking these days."

Jon takes out two bottles of beer with a palm tree and orange sunset on the labels and sets them on the countertop. He pops the lids with an opener and returns to the living room to hand off one of the glass bottles to Chaz. They clink the necks of the beers together, and Jon grins welcomingly. "Cheers, buddy."

Grinning, Chaz studies the label on the beer and nods. "Yes… To the next adventure."

They take a drink, and Chaz looks around the room. "Who's place is this? It's set up pretty nice."

"It's a friend of a friend's."

Chaz leans forward and glances down the hallway. "Not a bad place to base-camp, especially on this island. Anybody in the main house?"

"The local owner supposedly comes by on occasion. Haven't seen or met her yet."

The Navy SEAL raises an eyebrow. "Her?"

Jon grins and takes another swallow. "It's not like that. I haven't even met her face to face yet."

Chaz glances at Jon sidelong, with a simpering grin. "Kind of mysterious, eh buddy?" Jon shrugs and takes another short sip of his beer, while his old friend continues, "Any new adventures on the horizon?"

With a chuckle, Jon gazes to the foreign-stamped envelope on the coffee table. "Did you ever meet my friend, Lizzy Blackwright?"

"Was she the one from San Diego?

"Yeah."

Chaz's eyes light up at the recollection of a good story. "The treasure-lady, right?"

"Yep."

"I never met her, but have heard some of the stories."

Jon gestures to the small envelope on the coffee table with the foreign postmark and fancy handwriting. "She's on to something down in Jamaica and wants me to join her."

Picking up the thick card-stock envelope from the table, Chaz inspects it curiously. "Yeah?"

"Open it and take a look."

The beaming smile of the Navy SEAL widens, as he opens the envelope flap, takes out the handwritten letter and then the treasure map with the "X" mark on it. Amused, he looks up at Jon and then reads the short message.

Jon watches him examine the contents, takes a drink from his beer, and then snorts. "So, what do you think?"

Chaz finishes reading and looks up at Jon seriously. "Why aren't you there already?"

"I'm broke."

"So?"

"I only have a few hundred bucks to my name."

"When you first started out, that didn't hold you back from anything. You're getting soft with all your success."

Jon shrugs, as Chaz turns the envelope over to look at the postmark date. "Have you heard from her since this?"

"No... Nothing."

Chaz slaps the envelope on the palm of his hand and becomes animated. "This is a major adventure in the making. What are you waiting for?"

"I need some way to get down there."

"How about a boat?"

Jon nods and shrugs. "Yeah, I guess that would work, since Jamaica is an island in the Caribbean."

Chaz returns the nod, smiling with a telling wink. "Buddy, I can get you a boat. Get your stuff. I'll make a call."

Jon, sitting with his beer bottle balanced on his knee, glances over to his computer on the writing table and back at his enthusiastic friend. "Are you serious? Really…?"

"Yes, really… Shake a leg, Springer!"

CONCH REP

IV

The amphibious Grumman seaplane sits on the concrete slab a few yards from the ramp that slopes down to the water. Beneath the wing, ladders and a pop-up tent with a table full of tools and parts is set up under the disassembled left engine. The cowling is removed and pieces are scattered all around. Top mechanic, Ace Milton, with his arm buried to the elbow in the engine compartment, stands on a stepladder braced against the wing. He looks down at the display of components and his brow furrows as he inspects the torn-apart radial motor. "Sandy…?"

From the wide-open doors of the nearby airplane hangar, an attractive female in a skimpy bikini-top and cut-off jean shorts appears. Ace's aircraft maintenance assistant, Sandy, also has grease-stained hands and dark smudges of oil up to her elbows. She steps out into the sunlight and responds. "Yeah, Ace… What is it?"

Ace crouches down from his position on the ladder, looks at her and rubs the back of his hand across his cheek. "When are the rest of the parts due to arrive?"

"They should be here tomorrow."

The seasoned mechanic grunts. and shakes his head. "We should probably replace this ignition while we're at it."

Sandy steps below the ladder and adjusts her swim top. "Want me to look up the parts number and call it in?"

The old mechanic looks down at his assistant, with an advantaged top-view, but doesn't seem to be too distracted by her revealing outfit. "Yeah, see when they can get it out here. I'm going to start putting this engine back together… I just might have to do that another time."

With a friendly salute toward Ace, Sandy turns on a flip-flop heel and goes back to the hangar. "Aye aye, Captain."

~*~

Inside the apartment above the carriage house, the hand receiver for the antique rotary phone is hung up with a rattling ring. Chaz, pleased, turns to look at Jon. "It's all set."

"Yeah?"

"We have a boat ride to Jamaica."

"When does it leave?"

"We ship out this evening."

A bit skeptical Jon replies. "What kind of boat is this?"

Chaz gives a sly smile and tilts his head. "A tramp steamer headed to Ocho Rios. Once we're there, we can grab car transportation and travel toward Port Antonio."

Relaxing back in the club chair, Jon shakes his head. "The last adventure you took me on was a close-up tour of the Hollywood sign. That ended with us being escorted off the hill by a LAPD helicopter, ticketed, and put in front of a judge for trespassing."

Chaz grins at the humorous memory and shrugs. "I still regret getting caught on that one, but you had your sister along, so I couldn't ditch you both."

"I remember that all you kept saying was, 'Don't be the guy on the evening news who looks up at the chopper'."

The two have a laugh at the shared experience, and Chaz studies the details of the treasure map with the single, inked marking on the coastline. "What does the X mean?"

"I have absolutely no idea. Along with the note to join her, that's all she sent me."

Chaz nods his head and looks to the address again. "Oracabessa Bay, Jamaica? Hmm, you know, I think that's where Ian Fleming's Goldeneye is."

"The James Bond film?"

"No, his island house."

"There's an actual place called Goldeneye?"

Excited, Chaz's smile broadens. "Yeah, that's where Fleming wrote all of his Bond novels."

Jon stares across the room at his military friend, seemingly interested, but reluctant. "You think this is about some kind of James Bond treasure hunt?"

"Or maybe Errol Flynn's treasure… There were a lot of celebrity types that frequented the Jamaican paradise before it became notorious for ganja and reggae. Pirates used it as a home-base in their day, as well."

With a heavy sigh, Jon shakes his head dejectedly. "Let's try to avoid pirates on this trip."

Chaz grins. "How do you feel about buccaneers?"

"Isn't that the same thing?"

"I'd say pirate is a very loose term when it comes to some of my contacts in the Caribbean Islands." Jon stares at Chaz unenthusiastically, and the Navy SEAL swats at his arm. "C'mon, let's go grab some beer somewhere. Our boat leaves tonight at twenty-two hundred hours."

Rising from his seat, Jon heaves a deep breath and grabs a loaded duffle bag from the corner of the living room.

He puts it on the coffee table and looks inside. "My bag is still packed from my adventure with Fulton last week."

"Atta-boy… Keep that go-bag ready!"

Jon looks at his Navy SEAL pal and reluctantly nods. "Let me put a few things together, and I'll show you the local watering hole." Jon looks to his laptop computer on the table, back at the duffle bag and then up to his friend. "You'll like it. It's just the place where we can grab that drink."

V

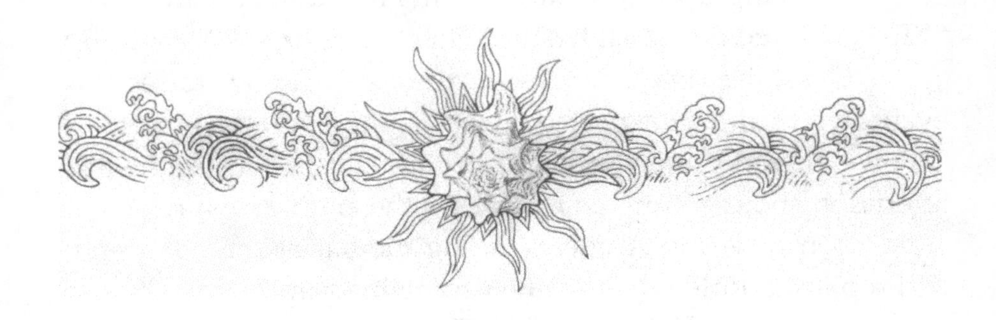

Jon and Chaz enter the Conch Republic Tavern. They make their way across the crowded barroom, which is still jam-packed with dozens of Ernest Hemingway look-alikes. Arriving at the bar after weaving through the khaki-clad gathering, Chaz can't help but smile, as he looks on at a pair of Papa-wannabes arm wrestling at one of the side tables. "What's going on in here?"

"The Hemingway festival is going on this weekend." Across the tavern, Jon spots the local seaplane pilot seated at the other end of the bar and calls out to him. "Hey, Rollie…"

The pilot pivots on his stool and waves the pair over. Once they break through the masses lined along the counter, the pilot shouts out just above the noise level of the crowd. "Hey, Springer. Sorry about that engine still being down."

Jon waits for Chaz to move up and introduces him, "Rollie McKinny, this is my good friend, Chaz Treadwill."

Rollie half-heartedly offers Chaz a hand, and looks to Jon. "He's not one of your Scott Fulton-type friends, is he?"

Chaz laughs loud and gives the pilot a firm handshake. "I'm more the type that gets folks out of trouble, not into it."

"Seems Springer here, could use more of those kinds of friends." Rollie grins at Chaz and laughingly turns to Jon, "Any luck on helping your lady-friend in Jamaica?"

Stepping up to the bar, Jon tilts his head toward Chaz. "We're booked on a boat heading there tonight."

Grabbing his beer from the bar, Rollie raises his eyebrows at the unexpected news of the sudden departure. "Wow, when did this happen? I just got a call from Angie this afternoon about getting an update on the engine repair."

Jon waves to Angie, working the bar at the other end, and replies to Rollie. "Chaz lined something up."

"What kind of a boat is it?" He takes a drink from his glass of beer and nearly chokes on it. "It's not Carlos, is it?"

The coughing fit grabs Chaz's attention away from the room, and he responds, "Who's Carlos?"

Rollie looks from Jon to Chaz and shakes his head. "He's one of those other types of friends we mentioned."

Chaz pushes out his chin, nods and replies, "Just a tramp steamer, heading south to exchange a load of goods."

Taking another drink to clear his throat, Rollie looks over the glass rim at Chaz. "It's going where you need it to?"

"Near enough. It will drop us along the north coast. We'll figure something else out when we get there."

Rollie shrugs and sets aside his pint of beer on the bar. "All right, that's good. Sounds like you have it figured out. The seaplane should be up and running in a few days, if there is a change to your plans."

After waving to Angie for a round of drinks, Jon pats the seaplane pilot on the shoulder. "Thanks anyway, Rollie. We should be down and back in a few days."

Still fascinated by all the literary look-alike characters filling almost every table in the saloon, Chaz turns to Rollie and asks, "What's this Hemingway festival all about?"

"It's a real fun time. Fishing, drinking and boxing. There will be a charity sparring match this weekend that I'm helping out with."

Rollie puts up his dukes, and then he bobs and weaves behind his fists while still seated on his bar stool. The Navy SEAL seems very interested in the mention of a fight. "Professional or amateur boxing?"

"Just pure fun, with a bit of scrapping for the masses… It's nothing like the bouts that happen on the sideline."

Chaz smiles. "Any money to be made?"

"Sometimes."

Jon takes freshly poured beers from Angie, hands one to Chaz and asks. "Are you scheduled to fight, Rollie?"

"Yep. I could get you on the program too. They got Aston lined up to show off some of his Papa memorabilia."

Impressed, Chaz takes a big swallow of beer and asks, "You know someone who sparred with Hemingway?"

The pilot grabs his beer again and takes a short sip. "Our pal Aston's dad was good friends with Hemingway when he lived here in the thirties. He showed Ol' Hem a thing or two about the art of boxing."

Beer in hand, enthralled, Chaz looks around the room. "I've never heard about any of this." He looks at them both. "You know, Jon, maybe we should reschedule our little boat-ride to Jamaica for another weekend?"

Holding his full glass of beer at chest level, Jon scans his gaze around to the crowd of socially-lubricated Papas. "We'll go check-in on Lizzy and should be back before the weekend festivities."

Chaz takes a gulp from his drink and smiles at Jon. "Sure thing… What could go wrong in the tropics?"

Across the crowded room, Jon thinks he sees the young, sunglass-wearing face of Casey Kettles peeking out from the back room and then ducking away. Glancing over the sea of celebrity impersonators, he puts the idea away from his mind, and resumes drinking.

~*~

The sun starts to dip low over the ocean horizon, as a pleasure yacht makes its way through the Key West marina. The personal yacht of Cuban businessman, Carlos Murrieta glimmers brightly, looking fresh and new after recent repairs to bullet-damage sustained on the ship's previous excursion. The yacht comes around from the north, through the marina, and pulls up at its usual slip, number nineteen.

Beyond the marina, in the adjacent parking lot, a large Conch-Cruiser automobile sits tucked under a grey tarpaulin. A gusting ocean breeze flutters the fastened fabric cover to reveal the bright yellow paint, chrome trim, and white-walled tires of a tucked-away 1960's Cadillac coupe.

As the luxury yacht is secured to the dock by an over-muscled seaman, Carlos steps out on the deck of the ship. Looking over the quiet marina and other ocean-going vessels, his gaze wanders to the twilight shadows along the harbor. He spots someone hiding near one of the shuttered tourist booths, smiles, and then draws a fat cigar from the breast pocket of his guayabera shirt.

Carlos licks the stick of tobacco with his tongue and rotates the stogie between his lips. He narrows his eyes in the coming darkness and takes out his lighter to flick the flame. After taking a few puffs from the Cohiba cigar he clicks the Zippo lighter closed and slides it back into his pants pocket.

Taking the cigar from his mouth and waving it toward the empty marina, he calls out, "Hello there, Mister Kettles."

Casey Kettles, still wearing his sunglasses, steps out of the shadows. He smiles at the man on the yacht's upper deck. The mischievous teenager leans casually on the boat-tour shack's wall and adjusts his sunshades in the evening light. "Welcome back, Carlos."

The Cuban businessman takes a few puffs from his cigar and pushes out rings of smoke from his rounded lips. "What news of the island do you have for me?"

The teenager holds up an empty hand and rubs his thumb and fingers together. With a beaming grin, Carlos takes a gold coin from his trouser pocket and flips it through the air for the juvenile informant to catch. Casey holds the valuable treasure coin up to the last rays of sunlight and scrutinizes it. He tests the softness of the metal by putting it between his teeth and biting. "Is this some of Mel Fisher's stuff?"

Carlos flashes his Cheshire grin and takes the thick, smoking cigar from his teeth. "*Was*, is the proper term. Possession is nine-tenths of the law."

The teenager shrugs indifferently and slips the coin into his back pocket. "That mainlander friend of Scott Fulton has another pal that's just come into town. There are whispers of a treasure hunt around."

The distinguished Cuban nods his approval regarding the information and thoughtfully takes a puff from the cigar. "Ahh, first pirates on the high seas, now treasure hunting? This writer-fellow should read more *J.T. Springs* paperbacks, to keep him out of trouble." Carlos leans forward on the deck rail and looks down at Casey, still standing in the shadows. "Good work, kid. Keep an eye on him, an ear to the ground, and let me know as things develop further."

The skinny teenager offers a feeble salute and steps back into the obscuring shadows near the tourist boat-ride hut. A haze of tobacco smoke drifts down from the yacht's high deck, as Carlos continues to puff on his cigar. He calls out to the muscled henchman working below on the pier. "Jorge, it's time to ready the Cadillac. I would like to make the rounds in town." He flicks a thick stack of ash from the tip of the cigar, and the end glows with a burning bright ember.

VI

The main tourist street of Old Town, Key West is full of people drinking, shouting and crowding the sidewalks. Several cars make their way down the street, avoiding intoxicated drinkers who occasionally stumble off the curb. Jon and Chaz walk through the throngs of tourists and turn to the street that will lead toward home. The Navy SEAL looks behind at the busy avenue, full of bars, and whistles low. "This seems to be a real wild town. How do you expect to get any writing done here?"

Jon looks ahead, down the quiet neighborhood street, which is in sharp contrast to the loud revelry going on behind. "I don't know if I've gotten much done so far, but there is something special about the island that sparks creativity."

"Anything like Los Angeles?"

Jon breaks into a grin, as he looks over at his friend. "Might even be better."

A pair of headlights cut across the dark street and veers in their direction. As the vehicle drives nearer, Chaz pushes

Jon aside to get them out of the projected path. "Watch out! That car is going to hit us!"

Both Chaz and Jon dive away from the road over a row of low bushes. A big, yellow convertible Cadillac bounces over the curb and comes to a rest, just short of the hedgerow the pair just leapt over. The bright headlights beam through the shrubbery, and Jon looks over at his Navy SEAL friend. "Dang, I think I know who that is…"

Standing up behind the low hedge, Jon and Chaz brush themselves off and stare into the glare of the car's headlights angled up from its canted position on the curbed sidewalk. Jon shields his eyes from the intense glare and calls out. "Carlos… Is that you?" The car shifts into reverse gear, revs the engine and backs off the walkway, bouncing down to a more appropriate position in the street.

The headlights illuminate the roadside, and a familiar voice calls out from the rear bench seat of the automobile. "Senior Springer… Glad to see you made it home safely."

Chaz follows Jon through the yard gate, and they both step out into the street. Still shielding his eyes from the bright headlights, Jon moves around to the passenger side of the car. "Hey Carlos… Trying to kill me on the open seas wasn't enough for you?"

Jon stands beside the large automobile, and Carlos reaches forward from the back seat to swing the door open. "Ohh, it's just a little local entertainment we Conchs have down here called *tourist bowling*."

"Tourist bowling?"

"Yes. It happens a lot along Duval Street."

Chaz seems too busy admiring the condition of the antique vehicle to be very mad about nearly being run over. Still upset, Jon glances over at the gorilla-like thug that is driving the car, and he has second thoughts about taking a swing at Carlos. "When did you get back to town, Carlos?"

The Cuban flips his small hand nonchalantly in the air. "Oh, just a few cosmetic touch-ups to our vessel, and we were back in order. All is in tip-top shape again."

"Do you mean the bullet-holes?"

Carlos shushes Jon with a wave and glances to Chaz. "A mere blemish is all. Who is your companion there?"

At the mention of bullet-holes, Chaz stops his inspection and moves around the car toward the open passenger-side door. "Hello there, I'm one of Jon's old research friends from the field, Commander Treadwill."

"Ohh, a Navy man?"

"Yes, sir. And who might you be?"

The Cuban extends his hand, palm down, as if Chaz was supposed to greet it like royalty, and replies formally. "Carlos Murietta, man of leisure, at your service.

"What kind of service is that?"

"Whatever is needed."

The Navy SEAL grabs the Cuban's hand, turns it and gives a strong handshake. "I will keep that in mind."

Carlos winces slightly from the military man's hard grip and slips his hand away to get the blood flowing again. "Hop in, and we'll give you fellas a ride home."

Jon shakes his head and steps back. "No thanks."

His Navy friend moves forward, puts a hand on the opened car door and interjects. "Actually, we need a ride over to Sugarloaf Key for a meeting tonight."

In the dim light of the vehicle's interior, the intrigued Cuban businessman scoots forward in his seat. "Ahh, a meeting at this hour of the night? Why fellas, it sounds like my kind of engagement."

Chaz remains outwardly casual and shrugs a reply. "You know how the Navy is. All work and no time for play."

Casting a noticeable look to his friend, Jon shakes his head subtly to decline the car ride with Carlos and Jorge. "We'll make it there some other way."

The Cuban pushes the passenger-side seat forward and gestures them both inside the roomy, classic automobile. "Welcome aboard, Commander." He smiles keenly at Jon. "Mister Springer here is something of a nervous passenger."

Chaz steps inside the car, to the rear bench, next to Carlos, and pulls the front seat back from its tilted position. "C'mon Jon. It'll be fine. Let's go."

"I don't know…"

"Why yes, Señior Springer… You probably won't get a better offer tonight."

Reluctantly, Jon climbs in the front and sits next to the hulking henchman positioned behind the steering wheel. "Hello Jorge." The ape of a man merely grunts and stomps briefly on the accelerator, which swings the heavy passenger side door closed with a slam. Carlos taps his hand on Jon's shoulder and leans forward to speak softly into his ear. "Where were the both of you going to… exactly?"

Chaz puts his arm up on the side of the car, kicking back to relax into the seat. "We'll let you know in a minute. First we need to stop by Jon's place to grab our bags."

The flamboyant Cuban settles back on the leather seat, swirls his hand over his head a few times and points ahead. "Onward, Jorge… To Señior Springer's place of residence." The driver watches his employer in the rearview mirror, glances aside at Jon and pushes his foot to the gas pedal again. The big Cadillac's engine revs and the car zooms forward down the dark, palm-lined residential street.

~*~

The front entry door of The Clipped Kitty opens with a quiet bell chime, and Casey Kettles enters the dark entryway. He shifts his yellow sunshades to the top of his head, tucks hair behind his ears and walks, barefooted, across the parlor. From one of the curtained hallways, the attractive features of the lady of the house, Giselle, poke out and smile at him. "Hello, Casey. Nice to see you home at a decent hour."

"What's up, Mama? Busy tonight?"

Stepping from the shadows into the greeting area, Giselle wears a revealing robe and nothing else but a smile. She replies affectionately to the youth. "I had them leave a plate of food out for you in the kitchen."

Casey cracks a trivial smile and gestures a thumbs-up. "Thanks, babe. See ya later." The teenager slips off down the pathway to the kitchen, leaving Giselle at the end of the hall. A man's voice utters something unintelligible behind her, and she turns to withdraw behind the thick, lush curtain.

Entering the brightly lit kitchen, Casey scoops up the plate of food set on the countertop. He continues on his way, picking off some cooked carrots and tossing them over his shoulder, as he walks to a door, opens it, and goes down another hallway. In a bellied-out corner of the hallway, a narrow door leads to a turret attached to the side of the house. Glancing over his shoulder at the trail of carrots on the floor, Casey opens the door and steps inside to a winding staircase.

Casey climbs to the top of the spiral stairway and comes to his bedroom at the upper portion of the small tower. The shining street lamps from Duval Street, a few blocks over, cast light through slim, curved windows and create shadows in the room. The teenager flips on a lamp and sits on the folded pallet of blankets and pillows that serves as his bed. Sitting cross-legged on the rumpled nest, he eats from the plate of food and chews quietly.

The light from the bedroom lamp reveals an odd collection of semi-valuable artifacts that have been pilfered from the pockets of the tourist population visiting Key West. On the dresser is a pile of cameras, and, in an open cigar box next to them, there is a collection of wristwatches of every shape, size and style. Casey finishes half the food on the plate and sets it aside on the blankets. He reaches into his pocket and pulls out the coin that Carlos flipped to him at the dock. Holding it under the light, he inspects the Spanish markings. After a while, he opens the nightstand drawer and drops it inside to a jar filled with other unique-looking coins.

Quietly chewing while gazing around the bedroom, Casey takes one of the digital cameras from the pile on the dresser and powers it on. The battery symbol in the upper corner flashes, as an electronic photograph fills the display. Scrolling through, Casey scans the photos of a happy family on their vacation trip to Florida. Photos from theme parks, beach time and other tourist destinations flash across the screen, as he observes a traditional family unit having fun.

Casey continues to stare at the digital photos, until the red-flashing battery indicator pulses and the images blink out. He tosses the camera aside and lies back on the pile of messy blankets. In the silence of his room, sounds from the main floor of the house are audible. The soft sound of a girl's laughter can be heard. Casey turns away from the light and wraps a pillow around his head.

VII

Under the dim tropical moonlight, a lone woman hastily packs a shoulder bag and suitcase. Distant car lights flashing through the wide, wooden slats of the plantation shutters catch her eye, and she quickly moves across the room to peek outside the window. The headlights flick off, and the distinct sound of car doors closing breaks the stillness of the night.

Through the slats of the window shutters, she can see several flashlight beams click on and move toward the house, scanning through the island undergrowth. The woman hears the chatter of insects quiet down for the moment, and watches the searching lights. She moves quickly across the room and grabs her backpack. Leaving the suitcase half-packed on the bed, she rushes out the back door of the house and slips into the darkness.

The bright beams of the handheld flashlights flick across the shuttered windows as they move nearer. Suddenly, the front door is forcefully pushed inward, and the twin streams of white light shine inside the abandoned bungalow.

One of the shafts of light flashes across the walls, while the other flashlight points directly to the open suitcase on the bed. The spotlight illuminates a label dangling from the handle that reads: *Elizabeth T. Blackwright*

The shaft of light lingers a moment on the luggage tag before sweeping over to the back door sitting slightly ajar.

~*~

A tramp steamer plows through the ocean waves, as it moves in a southerly direction. The early morning sunshine casts light over the blue waters of the horizon. With coffee mug in his hand, Jon steps out from the bridge on the aft deck. He looks out to the empty expanse of ocean and can't help but reflect on his recent boating experience a week prior.

Chaz comes out, stops alongside Jon, and notices his nervous contemplation. "What's wrong, buddy? Sea-sick?"

"I just had a bad experience out here not long ago."

Chaz looks down from the railing surrounding the bridge to the long shipping containers strapped on the deck. "Nothing to worry about. These guys are pretty legit now."

Jon glances at his Navy SEAL buddy, questioningly. "What do you mean… *now*?"

Chaz blows the steam from his own cup of coffee and takes a sip. "The captain is an old, Navy-school alumnus. Once upon a time, when he was just a crewman on this tub, they would smuggle square grouper to pay the mortgage."

"Fishing?"

The Navy SEAL laughs and almost spits out his coffee. "You being a big-time adventure-writer, you need to get out there more. I was referring to bales of marijuana."

Scanning the deck, Jon breaks into a nervous sweat. "What are they smuggling now-a-days?"

Chaz scratches the whiskers under his chin and shrugs. "It's probably nothing too illegal. That was back in the late seventies when it was easy cash, and everyone was doing it." The Navy SEAL casts his eyes over the cargo and continues, "Seems to me, I think he said this run was a shipment of resort supplies for the island. Supposedly he has a nice boat-load of Jamaican rum for the return trip to the States."

Taking a sip of his coffee, Jon can't help but laugh. "We're mixed up with rum-runners?"

"Well actually, we're tiny shampoos and hotel soap-runners on this trip. If we catch a ride back with him again, then we'll be into the good stuff."

Jon gazes out to the rolling waves all around them. "When do you think we will get to Jamaica?"

"Should arrive in port sometime in the late afternoon." Chaz glimpses behind to the ship's bridge and turns back to Jon. "I'll talk to him about picking us up in Port Antonio the day after, so we don't have to look for another ride."

"That will save us some time, but I don't really have the funds to help convince him to do anything out of his way."

Chaz pats Jon on the shoulder. "That's all right buddy. You're on my ticket for this one." He leans over and whispers. "The secret is to locate and secure some sort of cargo shipment that he can make a buck on to make it worth his while."

Jon nods appreciatively and takes another sip from his coffee cup. He stops when he suddenly realizes something. "You know what? I haven't even contacted my friend Lizzy to tell her that we're coming."

"Do you have a phone number to get ahold of her?"

Jon shakes his head dumbfounded and appears embarrassed as he replies. "No, I don't."

"Any other way to get in touch with her?"

"Not that I can think of…"

Cracking a mischievous smile, Chaz tilts his head. "She'll just have to be surprised."

VIII

On the island of Jamaica, the private beach bungalow has been entirely searched and ransacked. A gentle breeze blows in through the open doorway and scatters a crumpled pile of papers across the tossed interior. On the bed across the room, the suitcase has been dumped and rummaged through.

~*~

The steamship comes into port at Ocho Rios and ties off at the pier. Jamaican custom officials arrive to complete their paperwork, as the crew begins to bustle around the boat and prepare for the unloading of cargo. Each with a bag slung over their shoulder, Jon and Chaz descend the gang-plank and are met by the customs agent.

They hand over their passports and wait, while the Jamaican official carefully inspects their identification papers. He looks up at Jon, glances at Chaz and turns back to query, "What is your country of origin?"

Jon replies, "United States of America."

The agent nods. Then, he scans through Chaz's passport with its numerous pages filled with multiple travel stamps from all over the world. He peers up at him questioningly. "Mista Treadwill… What is yer reason for travel to Jamaica?"

Chaz grins and replies, "Tourism."

"How long will you be staying?"

"Just a few days."

Producing an official stamp from his shoulder pouch, the customs agent stamps each passport and hands them back with a welcoming smile. "Enjoy your stay in Jamaica."

The two Americans take their official documents and walk down the pier toward the town. Jon glances at Chaz and then over his shoulder at the customs agent far behind them. "I thought you'd have a travel-worn military passport?"

Continuing his quick stride, Chaz tilts his head and whispers quietly to Jon. "I have one of those too, but rarely use it for what they have me doing." Jon gawks at his friend, who merely shrugs and keeps walking.

"Okay. Where to now, Mister Special Ops?"

They approach the edge of town, and the Navy SEAL surveys the busyness of the small, tropical tourist port. "You're the one with the map… You tell me." Jon unslings his bag to take Lizzy's letter from his pack, and Chaz stops him. "Hold on… Don't get it out here. Let's wait for a better spot, where it is a bit less public."

Jon looks around at the lackadaisical Jamaican boatmen and dock crews and then to the crowded tourist shops. "You're thinking this might be hostile territory?"

Chaz lifts a warning eyebrow to Jon and smirks. "Always treating it like it is will help keep you alive longer." Jon slings his backpack over his shoulder. He follows his military pal down the dock to the village's fish markets, tourist shops and resort shuttle vans. Chaz diverts toward the parking area and explains to Jon, "We know that your lady-friend mailed that letter from Oracabessa, so let's hire a car and head in that direction."

~*~

The small port town of Ocho Rios is busy with its primary occupation of tourism. As Jon and Chaz stride away from the shipping dock and past resort vans waiting on souvenir hunters, they are greeted by a tall, slender islander with a wide, beaming smile and polo shirt with the name *Desmond* embroidered on the chest pocket. Instead of the usual-looking taxicabs and cargo vans, Desmond stands before a black Mercedes sedan that shimmers in the sunlight. "Haloo der, Mista Americas. You need a driver-mon?"

Chaz looks past the driver to the Mercedes and puts on an approving smile. "Yes, Sir! A ride to Port Antonio."

The driver nods agreeably and pulls open the rear passenger-side door. He motions them inside and exclaims, "Me name is Desmond, the driver-mon..." While smiling, he gestures to the name sewn on his shirt. "And, I can take you anywhere in Jamaica dat you please."

Jon nudges Chaz and gazes around at the lineup of more official-looking transports waiting along the avenue. "You sure this is the guy you want to be taking us around?"

Chaz shrugs and tosses his bag into the back seat. "Sure. Why not? He's driving a Mercedes... He must be okay." When Jon follows his buddy into the back seat, Desmond claps the door shut behind them and dashes around to the driver's side of the vehicle. Light on his feet, the Jamaican chauffeur jumps into the driver's seat, cranks the ignition key on the diesel engine and slaps the car into gear. "You both sit back 'nd relax der... Away we go!"

The black sedan tears away from the curb and leaps out into the flow of traffic, resulting in a blare of car horns from several angry motorists. Desmond turns his head, looks past his shoulder with a contagious smile and proudly proclaims, "I drive you real good, so just tell me where to go."

Highly entertained by the driver, Chaz puts his hand to the back of the seat in front of him and responds to Desmond. "Head toward Oracabessa for now, and we'll let you know the specifics when we arrive."

"Yes-mon, Sir!"

The sleek Mercedes zooms down the street through town and Jon looks out the dark-tinted rear windows at the crowded storefronts that are chock-full of consumer tourism. He looks forward out the front windshield, as the roadside quickly transitions to shaggy, palm-lined countryside with free-range livestock and small children playing on the curb. Chaz bumps Jon with his elbow and speaks quietly. "Okay, now is a better time for us to have a look at that map again."

Taking out the stamped envelope from his backpack, Jon removes the note and map and gingerly unfolds them. They both notice the driver's eyes flit to the rearview mirror. Chaz pushes Jon's hands down, lowering the parchment-paper treasure map out of sightline and takes the envelope from Jon. He looks to the postmarked address, leans forward to put his hand on the headrest again and speaks to the driver. "Can you take us to this address?"

When Chaz shows the driver the envelope, Desmond recognizes the local address and nods. "Ahh, da Goldeneye resort is next door. Yes-mon, no problem."

As Desmond returns his eyes to the roadway, Chaz sits back in the seat and tosses the envelope over onto Jon's lap. He looks to the adventure-writer and smiles. "Ya hear that? It's no problem, mon. It's next door to James Bond's place."

Jon holds the letter and envelope in his lap and exhales. "I don't want to discourage your enthusiasm about this trip, but Lizzy is often researching some boring, historical stuff."

Chaz gestures to the hand-drawn island map open in Jon's hand and shrugs. "Anything can start off an adventure. Has she asked you for any kind of help before?"

"No, I guess she hasn't"

All of a sudden, Chaz looks slightly uncomfortable and glances down to the decorative handwriting on the envelope. "I forgot to ask. Are you guys dating?"

Jon looks surprised. "No. Why would you ask that?"

"I just had the fleeting thought that maybe this wasn't about a treasure hunt at all, but instead an invitation to a romantic sort of getaway."

Jon shakes his head and laughs. "No, I don't think she thinks of me that way. It's all about work with her."

"You never know how a woman will figure things."

"Well, Lizzy is a pretty straight-forward gal."

"They all are bud. Until they're not... Then watch out." Chaz glances down at the map again and talks in a whisper. "Do you know what Oracabessa means in Spanish?"

"Something about a headwater?"

"Hmm, close... It means golden-head."

Jon looks up from the old map to his military friend. "You think there might really be some treasure involved?"

"When my ol' writing pal *J. T. Springs* is on vacation in the tropics and is mysteriously asked to come to an island-town named "golden-head" near the home of Ian Fleming, with an old treasure map included in the deal, I consider that a fine recipe for adventure."

Jon smiles and looks out the car window at the lush, island scenery scrolling past along Jamaica's coastal highway.

"I only write about this kind of stuff. Nothing like it actually happens in real life."

Chaz takes the map from Jon and studies it closer. "You'd be surprised what happens in real life that would never be believable on paper." He flips the treasure map over to study the backside, folds it carefully, and returns it to Jon. "Tuck that away in a safe place." He gestures to the letter inside the envelope. "That is our ticket to a new adventure, right there. Take care of it."

The driver's eyes flick to the rearview mirror once again, as the black Mercedes zooms down the two-lane road, following the coastline toward the fishing village of Oracabessa. Several car lengths behind them, another car rides up closer to the hind-end of a puttering, slow-moving motor-scooter. Swerving around the slow vehicle, the car seems to be staying within sight distance of the Mercedes ahead of it.

IX

The afternoon sun lowers in the sky over Mallory Square, as a cruise ship loads its passengers from the island of Key West. Throngs of people return from the restaurants and trinket shops, as street entertainers ply for their money and prey on the departing vacationers. Music and festivities fill the square while the cruise ship prepares to depart the port before the town's mandated time, prior to sunset.

Disembarking from a sailing vessel, a poised, blonde woman with aviator sunglasses breaks from the crowd. Elizabeth T. Blackwright has a scholarly, business-look to her in contrast with the multitude of tropical-shirt wearing vacationers. She has her shoulder bag slung over her arm, as she moves to one of the bicycle pedicabs dropping people off at the curb.

Climbing into one of the contraptions attached at the rear of a three-wheeled bike, Elizabeth puts her bag to her lap. The driver swings a leg over the seat and smiles back at her in the passenger box. "Just arrived? Where to?"

Elizabeth glances around at the flow of the crowd heading in the other direction and coughs to clear her throat. "I'm looking for a writer-friend that is supposedly in town. Where on the island would that type want to hang out?"

The pedicab driver crinkles his brow and contemplates. "A writer, huh? Probably drinks a lot… Beer or whiskey?"

"Beer."

"Is he straight?"

She smiles amused. "Yes. Last time I saw him, he was."

"I'd say the Green Parrot is a good one to start with." The driver puts his feet to the pedals, starts to push off and then pauses to look back. "Is he a big fan of Hemingway?"

"Oh, yes. Very much so."

Head tilted to the side, the driver nods and kicks off. "Then he's probably over at the Conch Republic Tavern."

~*~

The black Mercedes drives through the quaint village of Oracabessa, Jamaica. The road bends around a small bay, lined with several ramshackle fruit-stands, shops and the makings of a saloon. It takes only a minute for the car to cruise completely through the tiny community.

Jon looks out the back window at the insignificant fishing town they just passed through. "Not much there." Chaz looks out the window to the jungled side of the road opposite the water. "A lot of these island villages away from the resorts are like that… Just enough to support the community, and nothing for tourists."

Desmond looks into the rearview mirror and smiles. "Da address is right up here a few miles, right next to da Goldeneye resort. We be dar in a few minutes."

At the casual mention of Ian Fleming's Goldeneye, Chaz lights up with giddy excitement and asks the driver, "Any movie locations around from the original films?"

"Yes-sir-mon, da James Bond beach just o'er yonder. Da Honey Rider come up der as one fine-lookin' bikini lady." The Americans in the backseat exchange a juvenile grin, as they both form mental images of Ursala Andress, in a yellow bikini, carrying conch shells as she walks from the water. Passing an old wrought iron gate supported by a stone pillar on the left, Desmond hooks a thumb toward the driveway with a sign that reads: *Private Property.* He remarks to them. "Dat is da Goldeneye resort der behind dat gate."

With a mischievous smile, Chaz nudges Jon in the ribs. "We'll have to sneak you in there sometime, so you can sit at Ian Fleming's desk and get some good writer mojo."

Jon gives a chuckle as they pass the nondescript gate. "It looks more like the location where Bond would usually find the bad guys."

The car drives a bit further up the road, turns onto a driveway leading toward the coast, and winds down the narrow, frond-lined path. Desmond looks over his shoulder to his passengers in back. "Dis is da address on da paper."

Leaning forward on the front passenger seat headrest, Chaz peers through the windshield at the beachfront property. "There is a house up ahead. Take us up there, slow."

Desmond takes his foot off the gas pedal to slow the Mercedes to a crawl. The sound of tires crunching on the gravel path resonates loudly, as Jon rolls down his window to take a look at the dense, jungle foliage of the island property. He peers over Desmond's shoulder to see a brightly colored beach house with a white coral shoreline spread out beyond. "Nice place with a great view..."

The dark sedan stops in front of the quiet bungalow, and Chaz is the first one out the car door. He looks around, giving a low whistle of admiration at the exclusive location.

The bearded military man looks back at his friend and sighs. "You sure she didn't invite you with romantic intentions?"

Jon steps from of the car, with his bag, and looks to the manicured lawn surrounding the beach cottage veranda. Beyond the landscaped gardens and yard, the jungle seems ready to encroach. He walks the path to the front entry door. "I guess this looks like somewhere she would stay to work."

Chaz leans down to the open passenger-side window and passes their driver several folded American dollars. Smiling at Desmond, he puts his palms on the window sill. "You mind waiting a bit to see if our friend is still here?"

"No problem, mon."

"We might like you to come back again tomorrow and drive us all to Port Antonio, if you're available."

Desmond glances at the denominations of the folded-over bills from Chaz and beams an even wider grin. "I take you to anyplace on the island you want to go, my friend!"

Always preparing for the worse-case scenario, Chaz scans the long driveway and thumps the roof of the sedan. "Why don't you pull ahead and wait a few minutes for us. This looks to be a horseshoe driveway." The driver nods, and the black car rolls forward just around the corner of the driveway. Concealed by the thick greenery, the car shifts into park and cuts the engine.

Jon looks back at Chaz with his go-bag duffle in-hand. His hand hovers just above the door-knocker and pauses. "Well… Should we see if my friend Lizzy is home?"

Chaz ushers his hand forward. "After you…"

X

Navigating the milling crowds on the streets of Key West, the pedicab stops in front of the tree-shrouded courtyard of the secluded Conch Republic Tavern. Elizabeth steps out from the passenger box, looks around the quieter side street just off Duval, and hands the driver his fee. The driver stuffs the bills in his hip pocket and readjusts his Chicago Cubs ball cap. "The Conch Tavern is just in there. Over at the end of the courtyard..."

Elizabeth looks up to the massive banyan tree and the establishment tucked away from a clear view of the street. "Not an easy place to find."

"It's there for the ones in-the-know. Go on in and have a drink. If your friend isn't there, I'll cruise back around a bit later and pick you up. There are a few other places in town, if they haven't seen him."

"Thank you."

The driver runs a finger along the visor of his cap to salute and positions his sandaled feet on the bike pedals.

"Welcome to Key West Island. End-of-the-road America, where the weirdos go professional…" The bike cab pushes away from the curb and Elizabeth steps into the courtyard shaded by the huge tangle of branches from the ancient tree. She proceeds toward the secluded tavern entrance and pulls open the front door.

~*~

The sky beyond the Jamaican shoreline is starting to glow with the colorful rays of afternoon light. Nestled in the shadowed darkness of the jungle canopy that looms overhead, the beach bungalow seems strangely quiet and uninhabited. Jon gives a few solid knocks on the carved-wood door, and it swings open as if expecting their visit. He prudently looks back at his friend, and the Navy SEAL responds coolly, "Guess it's unlocked."

Pushing the heavy door open the remainder of the way, Jon steps inside to witness the messy ruin of the ransacked house. "Hello? Lizzy…?"

Standing outside the doorway, Chaz scans the room and switches to combat-mode. "This is not good. Not at all…" He unslings the military duffle from his shoulder and unzips a side compartment, as a car is heard coming up the driveway. Jon watches him dig in the gear bag and then peers out the window. "Didn't you tell our driver to wait?"

Chaz looks out the front door and sees the headlights of a car approaching from the entrance where they came in. "Different car, different folks." Chaz pulls a semi-automatic handgun from his bag and yanks back the slide to cock it. "Could be your lady-friend or could be the same ones who did the redecorating in here…"

Jon is wide-eyed. "Whoa, Chaz! What are you doing?"

The highly-trained Navy SEAL looks over at Jon with deadly seriousness. "You stay in here, and I will cover you."

Chaz pulls a camouflage scarf from his duffle and wraps it around his head as Jon stammers, "Wha… Wait…? What do you mean *stay here*? Where are *you* going?"

Outside the bungalow, the car stops short of the walkway and two men in dark-colored clothing step out. Despite the fading sunlight, they both wear black sunglasses. Jon gapes through the wide-open door and then back at Chaz. "I'm going with you."

"You have to stay here. We won't know what they want if one of us doesn't stick around to ask."

"Uh, you're kidding me, right? This is unreal."

"It's about to get real."

Jon pulls off his backpack and takes out the letter. "Here, take this in case they want to search me."

Staying below the sight-line of the shutter windows, Chaz takes the envelope with the map from Jon and moves quickly toward the back door. He pauses at the exit and looks behind to Jon before slipping outside. "See ya soon buddy… And don't forget to take some notes." Silently, Chaz disappears out the back doorway, as footsteps are heard on the front stoop.

~*~

Light streaming in behind her, Elizabeth steps into the Conch Republic Tavern. She looks around, admiring its old-world pub style and vintage charm. Descending the few steps at the entrance, she moves across the room to the lengthy bar. Gazing around, she can't help but notice there is more than most barrooms' share of Ernest Hemingway look-alikes. Everyone's eyes are glued on her, no doubt due to the fact that she strikes a beautiful Martha Gellhorn-type figure amidst a gawking sea of wannabe-Papas.

Elizabeth steps up to the bar and the patrons respectfully split away to make room for her. One of the

Hemingways leans in and clears his throat before speaking. "Can I buy you a drink, pretty lady?"

She looks him over, with his rosy cheeks and short-cropped white beard, and smiles graciously. "I buy my own, thank you, sir." The gentleman nods understandingly, and Angie approaches from behind the counter to wave him off. "Step back Papa… Give the lady some breathing room."

With a grin, the impersonator sweeps his thinning hair back and turns away from the bar with his drink in hand. Elizabeth looks to Angie, and the two women in the room instantly form a bond. "What is going on in here?"

Angie smiles and opens her arms wide to the room. "Hemingway Days are upon us again. It's a lot of fun, but it gets a little tiresome looking at the same face all week."

Elizabeth peers over her shoulder at the crowded room and swishes her hair back. "I wasn't sure what to think." Across the bar, Angie examines the newcomer and grins. "They were a bunch of sweet old fellas that turned into hungry wolves the instant you walked in the room."

Elizabeth turns back to face Angie. "How so?"

"The mere sight of a pretty blonde will put pep in their step, a tickle to their loins, and a flicker in their eyes."

"How sweet…"

The bartender kicks her foot up on something behind the bar and leans forward to speak privately with Elizabeth. "You sure did the right thing by refusing that drink, or they'd all be climbing over themselves to buy you the next one. Would be quite the macho brawl. What'll you have?"

Blushing slightly, Elizabeth sweeps back a strand of hair behind her ear and swings the bag from her shoulder to the empty stool beside her. "I'll take a Cuba Libre."

Angie nods and grabs a cocktail glass and a small lime. She mixes the drink and cuts the lime, as she scans around the barroom. "What brought you in this evening?"

"A recommendation on where to find a friend."

Angie squeezes a lime slice into the mixture and grins. "Does the lost friend have a white beard and wear khaki?" She slides the mixed drink over to Elizabeth and grabs an empty beer glass from the bar. When the older man nods for another, Angie grabs a fresh glass and pours a pint.

"He's a writer."

Angie glimpses over her shoulder with a funny smirk. "We get a lot of those in here. Especially this week..."

"He's a bit younger than most of tonight's crowd."

"What's his name?"

"Jonathan Springer."

The bartender finishes her pour and turns to set the draft beer before the waiting customer. She takes the money from the bar-top and looks to the blonde newcomer again. "You know Jon?"

"I'm an old friend."

Angie gives a chuckle and eyes Elizabeth curiously. "Jon is pretty new around here, but he seems to have a lot of old friends visiting regularly."

"Have you seen him lately?"

Angie thinks a moment, as she continues to study the female across the bar from her. "He was in just yesterday with another fella, who said he was an old friend, too."

Elizabeth breathes a sigh of relief. "I heard from his literary agent that he had forwarded my letter to Key West. I'm glad he is still here."

"Well, he is not here right now."

"I need to find him."

Taking another empty beer glass from the bar top, Angie gestures a wave to the customer as he moves away to the entrance. She turns back again and smiles perceptively. "Are you Elizabeth Blackwright?"

Momentarily shocked that an unfamiliar bartender would call her by name, Elizabeth hesitates from taking a sip of her drink and sets it down on the bar top. "Uh, yes I am…" She watches Angie gaze down to the end of the bar, and then put a hand up to stop Elizabeth from explaining further. Angie interjects, "Hold on… I got someone who can help."

As Elizabeth waits, the bartender goes away to find that certain someone. Scanning the room of bearded Papas, she sighs wearily and lifts her rum drink to finally take a sip. "It figures Jonathan would be mixed up with a roomful of Hemingways…"

XI

The front door to the beach bungalow opens all the way to reveal two dark-skinned Jamaicans in matching black outfits. Turning to face them, Jon stops in the act of pretending to examine a broken dresser drawer and tries to appear calm. "Hello, there. Can I help you?"

"Hallo der, mon. You expectin' somebody?"

"I was expecting to meet a friend."

The two silhouetted visitors standing in the doorway look around, and the one positioned behind remains silent. "You be here to meet da Missus Blackwright?"

Jon glances to the wrecked room. "Yes. Is she around?" He watches as the silent thug steps in, moves away from the door entrance and begins to make his way over to Jon's flank. The talker by the door puts on an insincere smile and replies, "We's here to take you to her."

Suspiciously eying the man skirting the perimeter of the room, Jon shakes his head. "I will just wait for her here. Maybe I will clean the place up a bit." The two thugs exchange a glance, and the one across the room from Jon steps closer. "We's been told to bring you to her."

Jon moves a few paces backward and replies, "Is she coming back?"

"Did you bring da map wit you?"

Jon looks aside at the quieter one, who stops inching closer momentarily when his eyes lock on him. "What map?" His gaze returns to the fellow by the door when he speaks. "Da Missus Blackwright, she says for you to come with us." The thug nods to the other one across the room, and Jon turns just as the quiet one starts to make a lunge at him.

Instinctively, Jon raises a clenched fist to punch out and connects at the cheek, near the bridge of the attacker's nose. Despite the solid smash to the face, the charging man's momentum carries him into Jon. They both tumble onto the bed, and Jon tries to push the temporarily dazed man aside, kicking the suitcase from the bed with a heavy thump.

Outside, Chaz observes the bungalow's front entrance while he remains concealed at the edge of the jungle foliage. As the light from the evening sky lessens, the view through the slatted window blinds into the bedroom becomes dimmer. He watches, as the thug at the doorway takes out a handgun. Jon suddenly pops into sight near the window and is instantly tackled from view by the other guy.

A gunshot snaps off inside the bungalow and birds scatter from their roost in the trees. Bursting from the brush, Chaz dashes toward the beach house with his pistol ready and murmurs aloud, "Oh, shit..."

~*~

Standing at the bar in the Conch Republic Tavern with her bag on the empty stool beside her, Elizabeth takes a sip from her cocktail. She turns to greet a man in a rumpled tropical shirt and khaki shorts, as he eases up alongside her.

He takes a swig from his bottle of beer and looks her up and down, seeming to approve. Offended by his examining gaze, she lifts her brow at him "Can I help you with something?"

He smirks. "I thought maybe I could be a help to you." Elizabeth looks at the half-drunk stranger curiously, until he suppresses a growling belch and continues. "Hi, I'm Rollie."

She stares at him with confusion, and he grins at her knowingly. Finally, she utters a remark to break the standoff. "So… Am I supposed to know who you are?"

Rollie grimaces, as if she should recognize who he is. "The pilot… Rollie McKinny. You need a drink?"

She raises her glass up slightly. "I already have one."

He offers an intoxicated expression and raises his own drink. "Yeah… Me too."

Behind the bar, Angie comes over and places her hand on Elizabeth's elbow. "Miss Blackwright, this here is Rollie. He flies airplanes."

"Yes, we've just become acquainted, and it appears he might be in for some sort of a wreck."

Rollie takes another swig from his bottle and smiles. "You know what they say about pilots…?"

Angie chimes in. "They don't like to go down?"

Not hearing the female bar owner's sarcastic reply, Elizabeth responds to the drunken inquiry. "What is that?"

"There are the ones who have had an incident, and those who will."

Elizabeth takes a sip and narrows her eyes at Rollie before she asks, "And which one are you?"

"Oh, I've had lots of 'em, all kinds, but they don't keep me grounded for long."

Rollie tips back his beer, finishes it off, and sets the empty on the bar. Angie takes the bottle and shakes her head at the tanked-up seaplane pilot. "Need another one, Rollie?"

The pilot smiles at Elizabeth and winks over at Angie. "Depends how things are going with Miss Blackwright here."

Elizabeth smiles at Angie and tilts her head toward the intoxicated pilot. "He might need another one to soften the crash-landing."

Angie leans farther over the bar-top and explains, "Rollie here was just talking with Jon yesterday."

Elizabeth turns to face Rollie. "You know Jonathan?"

"Yes, I do."

"Do you know where I can find him?"

"Possibly…" He hiccups and tries to compose himself. "Did you write the letter from Jamaica?"

Elizabeth turns from Rollie to Angie and finally realizes why they know her name. "Yes, yes, I did. Is he still around?"

"Nope."

"Where can I find him?"

"He's probably in Jamaica by now."

XII

Wrapped with twisted sheets in a grappling pose on the bed, the Jamaican thug and Jon look at the other man by the door. The smoking pistol in hand, he gestures the two off the bed. "You, dere! Let 'im go, 'nd get away from dere 'nd stand up.

Jon stops resisting and raises his hands high in surrender. "Don't shoot me. I give up."

The nonverbal thug pulls Jon away from the bed and touches his bleeding nose. He wipes the smear of blood on the bedsheets and pushes Jon toward the doorway. The Jamaican pokes the barrel of his semi-auto handgun at Jon and gripes. "Da next shot is pointed at yew. Give us dat map, mon."

Jon stares at the man and tries to decipher his thick Jamaican accent. "Dew, who…? Map, mon? I don't even know what you're saying?"

"Da map, mon!"

"What?"

The Jamaican thug raises the pistol threateningly and then suddenly tumbles to the floor, knocked unconscious.

Catching a quick glimpse of Chaz standing in the doorway, Jon feels a momentary surge of adrenaline. He spins on a heel and sends a driving punch into the mid-section of the speechless thug standing behind him.

Witnessing the man's stunned expression, Jon follows with another punch directly to the Jamaican's broken nose. The thug falls backward, and the lights go out for him before he hits the floor. Impressed, Chaz pops in through the doorway, gun ready, and whistles. "I'll be damned Springer… Didn't know you had it in ya!"

Jon turns to Chaz and wipes the knuckles of his hand. "I think all this Hemingway macho-stuff has my blood up."

Chaz takes the handgun from the man by the door and looks to the splintered wood of the bullet hole in the dresser. "Well, we best keep it that way. These boys mean business." The military man ejects the clip, tosses it away, then slide ejects the live round in the chamber. He tosses the rest of the gun outside into the bushes. "What did they say to you?"

"I think they have Lizzy."

Chaz holds up the letter and envelope with the map. "At least they don't have this."

The shock of the dangerous situation starts to sink in for Jon, as he watches Chaz pat down the other unconscious assailant in the room. He gives a nervous shiver when Chaz finds a small handgun on the guy he was just wrestling with. Jon stammers, "Crap…! I didn't know he had a gun when I swung at him."

With a smirk, the Navy SEAL looks up at his friend. "Would it have mattered?"

"Yeah, I think it would have…" As Chaz checks the load in the snub-nosed pistol and snaps the cylinder closed, Jon stares at him dumbfounded. "What do you plan to do with that?"

"Give it to you."

Chaz tosses the gun across the room, and Jon catches it with both hands. He looks down at the six-shot firearm and remembers back to the old-fashioned pistol lent to him by Rollie just a week ago. Jon looks up at Chaz inquiringly. "Dang, why do I always get the antique gun?"

Chaz tilts his head and grins at Jon. "You just look like someone who prefers a six-shooter to a semi-automatic."

Nodding in agreement, Jon examines the smaller gun. "What am I going to do with it?"

"Put it in your duffle in case you need it later."

Holding the handgun, Jon takes a deep, calming breath and drops it into his opened backpack. "Let's get out of here. You think our friendly driver is still around?"

Chaz shrugs and tucks his gun in his front waistband. "If he ain't, they had to arrive in some kind of vehicle."

Jon shakes his head and looks out through a window. "Are you kidding? We can't steal a car from these hoodlums."

Chaz laughs and nods toward the other end of the driveway. "His car was parked around the bend, last time I saw him." Chaz holds out Elizabeth's envelope and continues, "The gunshot might have scared him off." Jon grabs the letter, tucks it in his backpack alongside the firearm and leads out the front door of the bungalow.

They dash through the twilight shadows, noticing a Japanese import car at the entrance to the driveway, and continue toward the Mercedes parked around the corner. Chaz softly thumps his hand on the trunk, and Desmond pokes his head outside to smile at them both. "Tis a good ting ta see ya, Mistas."

Chaz moves alongside. "Thanks for waiting."

"Ya mon! But da next gunshot I hear was to be foot on da gas pedal for me."

Chaz swings open the door on the driver's side and slides in. Jon moves around the car and gets in the front. Desmond looks around at his passengers as they get situated and smiles at Jon. "Where to?"

"Let's just get the heck out of here." Jon clutches his bag on his lap, as the driver starts the car, pops it in gear and zooms ahead into the darkness of evening.

~*~

Exiting the Conch Republic Tavern, Rollie stumbles out into the night air and makes his way toward his pickup truck. Elizabeth follows behind him and looks down the sidewalk toward the big crowds on Duval Street, a few blocks over. "Mister McKinny, I can find my own place to stay tonight."

Rollie takes out his keys and rattles them in his hand. "Figured I would take you to the place where Jon stays."

Somewhat uncomfortable with the notion, she replies, "I don't think that would be proper."

"With the festival in town, you won't find much else."

"I'll find something."

Rollie thinks on it a moment then waves her over. "C'mon. There is another place that you could stay."

Elizabeth hesitates, in hopes of her prior pedicab making an appearance, and then follows Rollie over to his truck. "Are you okay to drive?"

Rollie stands up a bit straighter and smiles confidently. "Drive, yes… Fly, no."

She narrows a doubtful eye and puts out her hand for the keys. "I'll drive. Where else did you have in mind?"

The inebriated pilot notices her suspicion and smiles at her humorously. "I wasn't suggesting you stay at my place, if that's what you mean." He leans against the fender, hands her the ring of keys and points in her palm at the longest one for the truck. "Do you think you can drive this thing?"

Elizabeth opens the passenger side door and slides across the bench to the driver's seat. "If it has wheels and rolls down the road, I can drive it." She gives him a sultry smile and pats the dirty seat cover beside her. "Hop in, Honey." Rollie scoots into the truck and swings the passenger side door closed with a bang. He watches her press her feet to the brake and clutch pedals and start the truck. She glances over at him and grins. "Where to, flyboy?"

The seaplane pilot puts on a roguish smirk and replies, "I have a pal close by that has a bed available when I need it. She runs a place that's a bit like a boarding house."

Elizabeth shifts the truck into gear, and presses on the gas as she lets off the clutch. "Is it nice?"

Rollie smiles drunkenly. "It's heavenly…"

ROLLIE

XIII

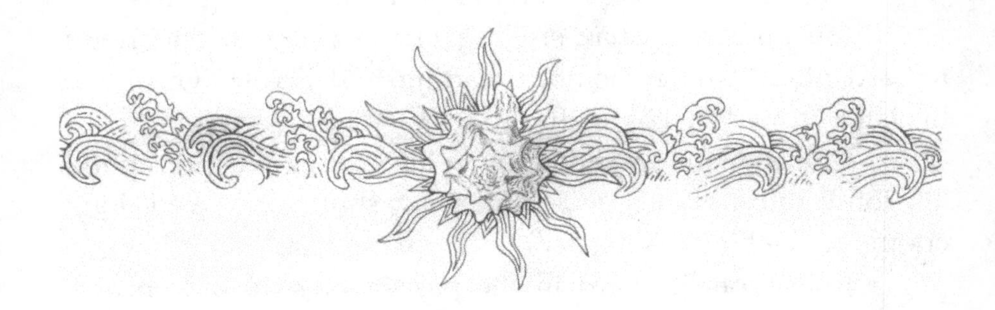

Back on the coastal road, the Mercedes sedan drives through the night. On one side of the highway, the passengers notice that several of the houses have lamps glowing in the windows and, on the other side there is complete darkness over the ocean. Instrument lights from the dash illuminate Jon's face, as he flexes his fingers and rubs the sore knuckles on his hand. Deep in thought, he reflects on the development of their difficult situation and his missing friend, Lizzy.

Desmond looks over at Jon and behind to Chaz. "Where to, Mon?"

Chaz pulls himself forward to the headrest into the light. "What do you think, Jon?"

Jon turns to Chaz and adjusts his position in the seat. "Port Antonio would be the next best place, I guess."

Desmond nods, and his smile beams bright from the dashboard lighting. "Da Port Antonio is a nice place to be. Long time a' go, was da place where da Mista Robin Hood came to live."

Jon looks at the driver to clarify. "Robin Hood?"

Desmond smiles and nods. "Yes! Da movie-star-mon, who swordfights in dem black 'nd white tight-pants and kiss all dem pretty gals."

Jon blurts, "Errol Flynn?"

"Yes, mon! In like Flynn to kiss all dem young girls."

Jon glimpses Chaz smiling in the backseat and turns toward him. "I do remember reading that Errol Flynn lived his later years down here after his career started to slide."

Chaz has that excited look in his eyes again and replies, "I don't think that good-timing swashbuckler lived long enough to let his career fade."

Jon pivots forward in the passenger seat and shrugs. "He died at fifty, but he lived a life worth twice as long." Sliding his backpack to the floor, Jon looks at Desmond. "Okay… To Port Antonio to find us a place for the night."

Smiling, the Jamaican driver maneuvers the Mercedes along the winding coastal highway. "Da port is a good place where my family has da Hotel Inn where Mista Flynn stayed with his lady-friends."

Chaz taps the back of the front headrest and smiles. "The adventures of *J. T. Springs* continue."

Jon frowns and peers back at his friend. "I hope they've changed the sheets."

~*~

The Key West Air Charters truck turns off the crowded street and makes its way through a quiet, little neighborhood. As Rollie gestures to a residence up ahead, Elizabeth slips the shifter out of gear and glides over to the curb. Stopping the truck in front of an ornate house shrouded by beautiful gardens, she notices the accented landscape lighting.

The sign on the mailbox next to the entry gate reads: *The Clipped Kitty*. Elizabeth studies the peculiar name and looks to Rollie inquisitively. "Is this an animal rescue?"

"It's not a veterinary clinic."

"Who lives here?"

"I know the lady of the house."

Elizabeth looks to the extravagantly restored historic home and nods her consent. "Okay, this should be fine." Rollie smiles to himself, amused, and slides out of the truck. "I'll introduce you, so they don't get the wrong idea."

She follows the pilot through the gate and along the path through the gardens. Before they reach the front door, she asks, "Why would they get the wrong impression?"

Rollie rings the bell on the door and a lower segment of the elegant, double entry doors opens at about his waist level. The seaplane pilot leans down, and Elizabeth can't quite hear what is said, but, after a moment, the spy-hole snaps closed. She stares, mystified, as Rollie puts his hand to the door and stands upright. "What did you tell them?"

The large doors slowly swing inward, welcomingly and Rollie ushers Elizabeth inside. "Just that a friend needs a place to sleep, and that I won't be staying myself."

"Have you stayed here before?"

"Uh, a few times… With friends."

Elizabeth pauses at the door and smiles at Rollie. "Thank you, Mister McKinny. For all your help tonight…." Handing over his ring of keys, she pats his hand appreciatively. Rollie returns her gesture with a gracious smile and takes a few steps back toward the front entrance gate. About halfway down the path, he turns and calls back to her. "We'll talk more about finding Jon tomorrow. In the morning, I'll send someone by to pick you up."

Elizabeth watches Rollie duck out the yard gate and get into his truck. The old pickup starts after a few cranks and rumbles off and down the street. As the sweet odor of perfume wafts out from the interior of the house, Elizabeth steps inside and murmurs. "What is a clipped kitty?"

XIV

The morning sun rises, as Jon and Chaz walk together along the road that passes by the harbor waters of Port Antonio. They approach the Errol Flynn Marina and gaze out at the various sizes and shapes of sailing yachts and fishing boats that fill the cove. Jon looks to his friend and wonders aloud, "What's our next step?"

Chaz takes his gaze from the marina and looks at Jon. "I talked with our driver's sister at the hotel's front desk this morning, and she is making some calls to get us a boat with some scuba equipment."

They continue their walk, and Jon glances over at his friend questioningly. "Why the scuba gear?"

Coming upon a café, Chaz nods toward empty chairs. "Let's sit and get some coffee."

"First rule of being a writer... Grab a drink."

Several blocks away, a Japanese import car carrying several figures hidden by dark-tinted windows cruises the busy streets. The car stops at an intersection and the people inside scan the pedestrians on the street before driving on. One of the men in the front seat has white tufts of cotton shoved up his nostrils to stem the bleeding of a broken nose.

~*~

Seated at a café, Jon and Chaz face out to the waterfront as two servings of steaming coffee arrive. Chaz leans forward on the table and inhales the hot aroma. He gazes around carefully and then looks at Jon, as he wraps his hand around the cup. Using a low voice, he seems paranoid. "I was looking at the map last night, and it appears that the indicated marking is near a small island not far off the coast."

Jon takes a sip of his hot beverage and nods, while glancing down to his backpack positioned next to his foot. "It's hard to tell, and it's not a good map for exact directions."

Chaz puts down his drink, then sits back and looks out to enjoy the ocean view. "I figure, if there isn't much to look at when we get out there, it'd best to have a peek below."

"You thinking that this might be an actual treasure?"

Chaz tilts his chin and smiles rakishly. "In water expeditions, all the good stuff usually sinks to the bottom."

~*~

The morning air in Key West is cool, with a hint of humidity that will become stifling by the middle of the day. Outside the Clipped Kitty, dampness fills the gardens after the watering system completes its morning cycle. With her bag, Elizabeth steps out from the wide front doors and looks down the walkway to the ornate gated entrance. As she approaches the twisted, iron gate she can see the rear wheel and fender of a bicycle on the sidewalk.

Exiting the elaborate domain, Elizabeth is promptly greeted by the welcoming features of the island sage, Aston. Mounted on his bicycle, he makes quite the first impression. His large parrot perches on his shoulder and his treasure-decorated, beach-cruiser transportation glimmers in the sun. "Halo der, Missus."

"Well… Hello to you."

"I's Aston and have been requested here to direct you, da Missus Blackwright, to da Mista Rollie at da Key West Air Charter place."

Elizabeth peers around the homeless-chic islander and notices that there is only a single bicycle for them to ride. "Umm, I wouldn't know the way."

The local character scoots forward on the long banana-style bike seat and nods his head. "T'is a good ting dat I do."

"How do you mean?"

He pats the space on the seat behind him and grins. "Hop aboard, lady. I take you dere."

She looks to the long, glittery cushion of the seat, with its sissy bar sticking up behind, and grimaces. "Oh, no, no… Mister Rollie said he would send me a ride."

Aston continues to grin and pats the long seat again. "Yes! Dat's me!"

The parrot spreads its wings, flaps them and squawks with laughter. "Hop aboard, hop aboard."

Sweeping a trailing lock of her blond hair away from her cheek, Elizabeth looks back at the gate of the Clipped Kitty and then to the junk-cluttered beach cruiser. "This is not what I was expecting."

"Dat's the way of life in da islands. Let's go."

"Okay…"

Approaching cautiously, she slides her leg over the seat behind Aston, grips her bag to her chest, and then props her feet up on a pair of conch shells that are used for foot-pegs. The islander pushes off from the curb and does a wide arcing U-turn in the street. Elizabeth leans back on the sissy bar while the bird flaps colorful wings, seeming to assist with the turning radius.

With a rattling clank of the bike chain on the gears, Aston pedals off toward Stock Island and the headquarters of Key West Air Charters.

XV

The usual street traffic of the Jamaican port town buzzes past, as Jon and Chaz finish up their morning coffee. Jon takes the now crumpled envelope from his backpack and smooths it out on the table. He stares at the fancy handwriting and thinks about his missing friend. “I can’t imagine how we’re ever going to find her…”

Chaz takes a swallow of his coffee and turns his head. "If we hang around long enough, she’ll probably just find us.” Troubled, Jon sighs and stares at the elegant hand-script on the envelope. Chaz kicks up a foot and relaxes back in the café chair, tapping his finger on the underside of the metal table. “What do you know of Errol Flynn and his time in Jamaica?”

Jon shifts his attention from the envelope and replies, “Not much, really. Only what I read about his own telling of it in his book, *My Wicked, Wicked Ways*…”

“You’ve read his biography?”

“It was an autobiography.”

Chaz nods and shrugs. “Wrote it himself, did he?”

"Yeah, and it's quite entertaining."

"I only know about him from some of the old movies." Chaz laughs. "What made you pick it up?"

"I thought it was required reading when you live in Hollywood long enough to call it home."

Chaz thinks aloud, "Did he write anything else?"

"He wrote some war correspondence during the Spanish Civil War and various things in Cuba about Castro. His other two books were sailing-adventure stories from where he grew up in Australia and the South Pacific."

"Did he ever hunt for treasure?"

Jon is quiet while he thinks over Flynn's writing career. "In his first novel, *Beam Ends,* which I heard was semi-autobiographical, he looks for treasure in New Guinea."

"How about his other book?"

"I think he was after a woman."

"Makes sense…" Chaz smiles and contemplates aloud, "A few years ago, I met an old-timer in Leadville, Colorado, who liked to pan for gold when he was a youngster."

"Yeah… Okay?"

"Do you know what he liked to do when he got old?"

Jon shrugs a reply. "Chase women?"

"Yeah, that too." Chaz chuckles and nods his head. "But, he still enjoyed panning for gold in the high-country."

Looking out at the many sailboats in the port, Jon stares to where the rolling blue waves meet the horizon and beyond. "You think this is some of Errol Flynn's found treasure?"

"It could be. The map looks to be less than a hundred years old, so it wasn't from Blackbeard's time."

Jon taps the envelope on the tabletop and slips it back into his backpack. "I don't really know anything about it."

Chaz leans forward on the table and whispers to Jon. "Why wouldn't a rich movie-star from Hollywood, who looked for treasure as a kid and had his own sailboat, not want to play Treasure Island here in the Caribbean islands?"

Jon gazes around and then waves the waitress over to their table. As she approaches Jon smiles at her and then asks, "Excuse me, is there a library nearby?"

The waitress tilts her head and points down the street. "Yes, mon, just ov'r dar, on dat street by yonder, is da ol' Portland Parish Library."

After they both take a moment to decipher her strong island accent, they smile at her and nod. Chaz reclines back. "Thank you, we'll pay now." With a beaming smile, the waitress tears off a ticket, sets it on the table and saunters off. "Why the library?"

"I want to take a look at some local history."

"About Flynn?"

Jon nods with a shrug. "It's a good place to hide out, and maybe we can connect some of these dots."

"Good idea. I should probably start looking into some sort of plan to get us back stateside, as well."

~*~

With his reluctant passenger, Aston pedals his bicycle through the entry gate of the chain-link fence that surrounds the seaplane base. They ride past the amphibious airplane, parked above the water ramp, to the open hangar doors. Elizabeth looks to the paint-faded logo over the big door that reads: *Key West Air Charters – Adventure, Danger, Romance.*

She slides off the cruiser bike and murmurs to herself, "Sounds like a recipe for disaster."

Appearing from the shadows inside the hangar, Rollie comes out with the same clothes on from the previous night, only more rumpled. "Hello. Good morning, Miss Blackwright. Sleep well?"

Elizabeth watches him approach and smiles kindly. "Despite the old plumbing, grunting and moaning all night, and the wind seeming to ring the bell on the door constantly, it was a pleasant stay."

Slightly embarrassed, Rollie flushes red and looks to Aston on the bicycle. "Thanks for picking her up."

The islander combs his tangled hair back, smiles and kicks the stand to prop up his bike. "No problem, Mista Rollie. It is always a good day to have a nice lady along for a ride."

The seaplane pilot looks over to Elizabeth and asks, "Forgot to ask you last night... Did you come to Key West directly from Jamaica?"

"Yes, I hitched a ride on a sailing yacht."

Rollie turns back to Aston, who stands next to his bicycle stroking the soft, tail feathers of his parrot companion. "When is the last time you've been to the island of Jamaica?"

"Let's see... They booted me from the island in da late seventies, and I haven't been back der since."

Staring at the pirate-styled eccentric, Elizabeth's eyes go wide. She utters, "Kicked out of the country forever?"

Aston continues to smooth his hand down the feathers of his pet bird and smiles. "When the judge-mon asks you to leave da island, and says he will throw away da key if he sees ya der again, it feels like for good."

Nodding with sympathy, Rollie turns back to Elizabeth. "I made a call this morning, and it sounds like Jon and a friend probably arrived in Ocho Rios yesterday."

"What friend was he with?"

Rollie smirks. "It wasn't Scott Fulton."

Elizabeth sighs with relief and replies, "I hope it wasn't one of his other adventure-loving pals."

"I think his name was Treadwill."

She takes a calming breath and seems like she might go weak in the knees. "This shouldn't have happened."

"That's the way things go sometimes."

"Yes, but he's in danger there."

Rollie notices her change of complexion and ushers her to the cooler shade inside the hangar doors. "Are you okay, Miss Blackwright? Come in here and have a seat."

"Why is he in Jamaica?"

Rollie waits until she sits down and asks the woman, "Didn't you write him to join you?"

"Yes, but that was before."

"Before what?"

"Well, before those mafia men came to take this…" Elizabeth opens her shoulder bag and takes out a gold skull.

Despite her position out of the sunlight, a detailed carving of a map can be discerned on the tarnished cranium. Rollie stares, baffled, at Elizabeth holding the golden treasure and utters, "Damn… What is that?"

"The map I sent Jon was just to convince him to come and visit. All was in good fun, until I actually found this."

As Aston steps forward, his hand rises up and impulsively reach out to touch the golden skull in her lap. Elizabeth watches him curiously, as the islander speaks as if in a trance, "That isn't just a treasure… That is da map to da mother lode of fortune."

"You know of it?"

"During my time in Jamaica, I spend more'n a few months diving in the ocean searching for it myself."

Rollie observes the pair of treasure-enthusiasts, while they bond over the mutual pursuit. Elizabeth looks up and glances back and forth between the two men, then explains. "The map I sent Jon marks the island where Errol Flynn supposedly had a beach hut off the northern coast of Jamaica.

He used the shack as a home base to take his boat, Zaca, out to search for pirate treasure."

"Let me guess… He found some?"

"I found this near Port Antonio, where there are several remnants of scattered shipwrecks."

"So?"

Aston removes his hand from the gold skull, breaks from his trance and cautions them. "There are those who strongly believe in da lost riches of dat island. If the writer-man looks in da wrong places too much, he may get mixed up with da Jamaican Booty Posse."

Rollie lowers his chin at the funny-sounding name. "Booty Posse?"

Aston nods his head slowly and remains very serious. "Da gangstas down der in Jamaica have some bad names, but dey mean serious business. Some do guns 'nd ganga, others do coke 'nd crime. Da Booty Posse is all about lost treasure and antique artifacts on da black market."

The seaplane pilot looks to Elizabeth for some answers. "Is any of this sounding familiar?"

She nods her head, guilt-stricken at the mention of it. "I've researched some of the mafias in my studies, but I didn't have much to go on until I found this. Jon was supposed to come visit me, not get mixed up in Jamaican gang violence."

Looking over to his parked seaplane, Rollie lets his eyes linger on the recently repaired engine and the curved nose pointing out above the water ramp. "I guess we better go and get him." Aston pushes his ride to the shade and lifts his parrot from his shoulder onto the high handlebars of the bike. "Yes, Rollie-mon. I better go with."

Mystified, Elizabeth looks at the odd pair and asks, "What are you two actually considering?"

Rollie shrugs his shoulders and offers a wry smile. "We'll just swoop down there, grab Jon and his pal, and be back for the Hemingway festival by the weekend."

Unsure, Elizabeth looks at Rollie. "We can do that?"

"As long as we don't get caught."

Key West

XVI

The exterior of the Portland Parish Library is not the classic, well-built structure typical of literary institutions in America. This den of knowledge is housed in a squat, yellow and green-painted brick building with cages on the windows and a barred security entry at the front door. A small group of vagrants plays dominoes under the palm trees, as Jon and Chaz walk past to scrutinize the derelict facility. Jon winces at the sight of the primitive security measures. "Looks like a county jail or something."

"I've seen worse." Chaz exchanges a look with Jon.

They proceed to the gated entry while a tropical bird squawks from a treetop. Creaking on the hinges and banging shut, the door to the library building closes behind them as a black Japanese import car pulls up across the street and stops. Inside the car are four local men, dressed in dark clothes, two of whom had greeted Jon and Chaz the night prior.

~*~

At the Key West Air Charters base, the dual overhead seaplane engines backfire and then rumble as they throttle up. Spinning propellers blow sandy grit from the parking area, and the Grumman seaplane rolls forward on the water ramp. The dual engines thunder and growl in unison while the seaplane noses into the shallow water and begins to float. Splashes of waves ripple behind the whirling propellers and the amphibious vessel cruises out to deeper water.

The wheel struts on the flying boat slowly retract into the curved hull, and the engines begin to increase with power. Spray blows behind, as the seaplane charges forward, gets up on the step like a winged powerboat and then lifts skyward. Mists of water cling to the bottom of the airborne seaplane, as it banks south toward Jamaica.

~*~

The keys of an old, yellowed computer keyboard click away, and Jon watches the cursor blink on the green monitor. Across from him, sitting on a decrepit, fabric-patched chair, Chaz looks through an old, dusty volume on Jamaican history. Jon scans an article on the computer screen titled: *Movie-Star Adventurer comes to Port Antonio for Pirate Treasure.*

Reading through the slightly-blurred, digitized newspaper print, he jots down a few notes on a scrap of paper. After perusing the article, Jon types in another search which brings up only a few entries. He clicks on one of them, as Chaz comes over with his book on local history.

The Navy SEAL places the open book on the computer desk next to Jon and points his finger midway down the page. "This is what you should look for if you want lost treasure."

Jon looks at Chaz and then down to the book and reads: *"Mother Nature takes Revenge on Wickedest City in the World."* He glances up to Chaz, and then he continues reading.

June 7th, 1692 - earthquake at Port Royal – A 7.5 magnitude earthquake hits the island city built on sand which instantly liquefies some 33 acres of the city. As buildings slide into the ocean, geysers erupt from the earth and fort structures collapse. Shortly after, a tsunami wave washes the remainders out to sea. Among the death and destruction, the cemetery where Captain Morgan, the former Lieutenant Governor was put to rest, slipped into the sea and the skeletal remains of the long departed were mixed with the recent deaths from the pirate town.

Jon looks at Chaz again and curiously lifts an eyebrow. "You think that was the treasure Lizzy was looking for?"

"The whole city fell into the ocean. I imagine there were more than a few treasures that went in along with it."

Taking out Elizabeth's letter, Jon slides the map from the envelope and looks at the location of Port Antonio on the northern coast and Port Royal on the southern peninsula under Kingston. He turns his gaze to Chaz and comments, "The marking on the map is up here near to where we are. That earthquake happened on the southern part of the island."

Chaz studies the map over Jon's shoulder and shrugs. "It's been over 300 years. Things get moved, treasure gets looted and redistributed all over the world. There's no reason some if it wouldn't be stashed on this side of the island."

"What kind of treasure items are we looking for?"

Chaz looks around at the few local faces in the mostly empty library. "I don't know, but we should check at the hotel and see if our boat ride is ready to get us out there."

Jon slides the folded map back into the envelope and then stuffs it inside his backpack. He clicks off the search page on the computer screen and pushes back in the library chair. "Okay, let's see what we can find."

~*~

The flying boat soars over rolling patches of blue-green ocean water. Looking out through the windscreen, the faint form of an island coast appears in the haze on the horizon. Seated at the left seat controls, Rollie reaches up with his right hand to fine-tune the individual levers of the engine throttles. Next to him, in the co-pilot chair, Elizabeth adjusts her headset on her ears and speaks in the attached mouthpiece. "Is that Cuba up ahead?"

"Yeah… We'll have to stay low to keep under their radar or go the long way around."

Aston pokes his shaggy head up from the back cargo area and strokes his fingers through his long beard whiskers. "No fly-over permit needed when ya go for tourism."

The pilot glances over his shoulder and shrugs. "Yeah, but you have to file a flight plan and usually ask 'em first." Aston smiles and gives Rollie a pat on the arm. "Dat's okay. Fine with me. I don't even have a passport anymore."

Bewildered, Elizabeth looks with at the seaplane pilot and the bearded islander poking his head into the cockpit. "What kind of operation are you guys running here?"

Rollie shrugs, nonchalant, and then pushes the yoke forward and flies the plane down to an even lower altitude. "Seems I'm on the 'Jon Springer rescue mission' once again." The passenger in the co-pilot seat hooks her thumb to Aston standing between them and asks, "How is he going to make it through customs in Jamaica if he doesn't have a passport?"

"We'll have to drop him offshore somewhere first. After we do a customs check at Ian Fleming International, east of Ocho Rios, and are clear, we can pick him up again and then find Jon and his pal."

Elizabeth's eyes light up and sparkle with intrigue. "Wow, I really had no idea that Jon was running with such an adventurous crowd…Just like in his stories!"

The pilot grins and glances over at her. "He said he was making a go at the writing thing. Has he written any books?" She looks at Rollie and seems very surprised by the question. "Uh yes… At least a couple dozen."

The seaplane pilot returns his attention to the island of Cuba on the horizon, which they are quickly approaching, and drops their altitude, lower on the deck over the rolling waves. "Hmm, he hasn't mentioned them."

Staring out the forward windows, Elizabeth pushes back in her seat and watches, as they dive to a few hundred feet over the water and roar toward the nearing landmass. "Are we worried about the Cuban military?"

Rollie reaches up and adjusts the engine throttles. "Only if they spot us…"

The high-winged Grumman seaplane flies low, just above the wide sandy beach, and roars over the jungle trees. Rollie seems to enjoy the close-up action of flying near to the ground, as they follow the contours of the rural terrain below. Peering out the window, Elizabeth looks down at the tropical island below. "It really is a beautiful place."

Rollie smiles and nods in whole-hearted agreement. "Yeah, Cuba is definitely a diamond in the rough… Now for the tree-top-flying part of our tour!"

Port Antonio
Port Royal
N
W
E
S
CARTE DE L'ISLE DE
LA JAMAIQUE

XVII

Walking up the set of stairs to the Hotel Inn in Port Antonio, Jon and Chaz move around a homeless-looking man seated midway on the steps. Jon catches a glimpse of dark features, covered over with long, silver twists of dreadlocked hair. "Excuse us, sir." The old man looks up with icy-blue eyes and mumbles something in a local accent that is unintelligible.

They enter the hotel lobby, and Jon glances at Chaz. "Did you make out what he said?"

"I have no idea."

At the hotel's front desk, Chaz takes the lead and smiles kindly to the ebony-skinned girl behind the counter. "Hello there, darlin'. Any luck finding us that boat and gear?"

The young Jamaican girl beams with a pearly-white smile and looks down at the page of her notepad with scribbles of writing on it. "Hallo, der. Yes-sir, Mista Treadwill. My brodder, Desmond, says for you to meet at da Errol Flynn Marina at noon for da trip on da boat."

Chaz nods to Jon and turns to the girl at the counter. "Was he able to find some scuba gear for us?" She nods and looks proudly from Chaz to Jon. "Ya, mon. All lined up with da gear from Lady G'Diva Scuba Company."

Tapping the counter with two fingers, Chaz nods. "Thanks darlin'." He looks down at his military-style wristwatch and then over at Jon's very expensive timepiece. "Okay Springs, let's synchronize our watches for a boat ride at twelve-hundred hours."

The girl behind the desk keeps her smile and inquires, "Oh, are you da American, Mista Springs?"

Jon looks at her curiously and hesitantly replies, "Yes?"

She hands him a slip of paper with several notes and the times jotted alongside it. "Da Mista Moselly called for you many times and left lots of important messages. He says to phone as soon as you is able. Der is a lobby phone by dem chairs o'er der." Jon reluctantly takes the note and reads the long list of messages from his California literary agent.

Chaz peeks at the handwriting. "Anything important?"

"Not really."

"You sure?"

"I'll call him later."

Chaz moves away to the main stairway in the lobby. "Let's go upstairs to our room, gather some things together, and head over there early." Jon tucks his agent's note into his pants pocket, while he follows Chaz to the stairway.

Midway up the stairs, Chaz stops and turns to look out the front entryway. He studies a car parked across the street. Jon comes up from behind, and they continue on to the second floor. Keeping his voice low and speaking over his shoulder, Chaz comments. "Hey buddy, that fancy wristwatch of yours may get you celebrity status in Los Angeles, but it might find us the wrong kind of attention down here."

Looking down at his luxury watch, Jon grimaces and nods in agreement. "Yeah, that's a good point." He pulls his wrist to his abdomen, unclasps the timepiece, slips it off and tucks it away with the list of phone messages in his pocket.

They reach the top of the stairway and step out into the main hall. Chaz notices that their room door is slightly ajar. He extends his arm out to shield Jon and moves slowly down the corridor. "Stay back behind me..."

Approaching the partly-open door, Chaz reaches out and gently pushes it a bit further inward. Clenching his hand in a ball, ready to strike, he peers inside. Suddenly, he relaxes his tight fist and takes a relieved breath. Jon looks past Chaz to see a woman in their room, dressed as a maid, making up the beds. He whispers quietly to Chaz. "Hey buddy, are you going to kick her ass?"

The military man looks behind to Jon and smiles. "Nope, but we should probably take all our important stuff with us when we catch that boat."

~*~

The Japanese import car, with the four thugs inside, sits across the street from the hotel with the engine still running. They get a hand signal communication from the old, homeless man lazing on the stoop and slowly cruise down the street. The car stops at the corner grocery, and the thug with the white medical tape on his busted nose gets out and goes to a decrepit pay phone mounted on the outside wall.

After digging in his pocket for some loose change, he drops a few coins in the slot and punches a number into the worn keypad. He whispers a few words and then glances down the street to the hotel, as he listens to the voice at the other end of the line. Nodding, the thug looks to the others in the car and back at the man on the steps of the hotel.

He bobs his head again and hangs up the telephone. Stepping to the car, the man opens the passenger side door, slides inside and gestures ahead to the end of the city block. The car drives slowly forward and passes a large, billboard sign for: *Errol Flynn Marina.*

~*~

On the walkway leading to the Errol Flynn Marina, Jon and Chaz carry their travel gear while scanning the various seagoing vessels. The harbor has a long wooden dock that extends out into the water, providing berths for several large sailboats and a few luxury cabin cruiser yachts. An offshoot of the marina, with spots for the smaller fishing and local boats, juts to the side.

The mid-afternoon heat and humidity increases as the pair walks the planks of the pier searching for their hired vessel. A whistling call from one of the fishing-style cabin cruisers turns their attention, as the dark, short-napped head of their car driver, Desmond, pokes out a port-side window. "Hallo der… Da traveler-mons. Dis is da boat dat you hire."

Jon and Chaz walk up to the tethered, old-school, wooden fishing vessel. Jon nods his approval to Desmond. "You gonna take us out?"

"Yes mon. I's the captain 'n driver-mon in one package. All geared 'nd gassed up. I even have some of Mama's jerk chicken along for da snackin'."

Jon climbs aboard, tosses his pack aside and watches, as Chaz takes a last, lingering look down the dock before jumping aboard the forward deck of the boat. Chaz calls out. "Looks good. Let's take 'er out."

"Aye aye, mon."

The driver, turned boat skipper, moves forward to untie the dock lines and then releases the rope from the stern. Drifting from the berth, Desmond positions himself at the ship's wheel and controls before starting the diesel engines. The fishing boat kicks out a big cloud of exhaust, gives a healthy rumble and pushes forward away from the pier. Steering around the other boats, Desmond points the bow out toward open water.

Seated on the padded bench seat at the starboard side, across from the sport-fishing fighting chair, Jon looks to the piles of scuba gear and diving tanks lined up along the stern. He takes the letter from his backpack and examines it again. Turning it over in his hands, he can't help but think of his friend Lizzy and the trouble she has found herself in.

As the fishing boat cruises steadily out of the harbor, Jon slides the map out of the envelope. He unfolds it carefully and looks to the X marking placed just off the shore of a coastal island beyond the peninsula with the Port Antonio lighthouse. Chaz walks over, puts his foot up on the bench next to Jon and looks at their current position on the map. "Where to now, Captain?"

The adventure-writer looks up at his friend and points to the spot marked with the X on the old map. Gesturing a wave toward the uninhabited landmass offshore, he replies, "Our destination is marked for somewhere on the northern coast of that small island."

The fishing boat cruises out from the sheltered bay into the rocking waves of the offshore waters. The two old friends turn to watch the view of the marina slip away behind them. Holding on, to keep his footing, Chaz calls to their boat driver. "Desmond, let's begin with a cruise around that island."

"Aye aye, mon. Navy Island it is!"

XVIII

The rented fishing boat is just leaving the mouth of the island harbor when a pleasure yacht starts up and backs away from the crowd of boats at the dock. The big cabin cruiser has dark-tinted windows that obscure the number of occupants inside. The intimidating vessel rumbles across the bay, following the path of the smaller boat.

~*~

Flying over Cuba, the Grumman seaplane remains only a few hundred feet above the ground. As it roars overhead, flocks of birds flush out from the dense jungle trees below. The seaplane stays low and level, until they fly over the opposite coastline and to the open ocean again.

Rollie grins at Elizabeth. In response, her eyes sparkle, and she returns his smile with a reply over the headset radio. "That was a very unusual experience."

"We aim to please."

"Which part of your company motto was that?"

The seaplane pilot laughs, readjusts the microphone on his headset and replies. "That one was definitely *Adventure*. We try to save *Danger* and *Romance* for later in the flight, after the snacks are served." The rumbling engines continue to thunder and vibrate through the airframe, as Aston pokes his head forward again. "If we've made it past Cuba okay, I guess dis is da time for a Jamaican plan?"

Rollie peers past his shoulder to Aston and tilts his head. "You have any ideas where to drop you before our stop at International Customs?"

"Der is a small island I know of. As we come in from da north, we should be out of sight from the mainland."

Rollie takes out a nautical boat chart of the Caribbean islands and hands it back, over his shoulder to the passenger. "Give me the coordinates and we'll make that our first stop."

Elizabeth looks beside at the pair with their ocean chart and lays her head back to relax for the remainder of the tour. "I guess *Danger* is next on the itinerary?"

~*~

Away from the Port Antonio harbor, Desmond steers the fishing boat to the east and around Navy Island. They cruise the island coast, until they come around to the north shore where the clear, shallow water reveals sandy shoals. Desmond slows the boat, holds the ship wheel, and waves his arm out to greet the uninhabited isle. "Dis is da Navy Island. Named for da place dat da English ships rolled their boats in da shallows ta clean off da bottoms."

Chaz gazes over the side at the varied depths of water due to the sandbars and coral reefs. He looks at Jon and nods. "If you could actually steer one of those big sailing ships in here, the trick would be getting it out again."

Jon peeks over the railing of the boat and responds. "Yeah... I guess the tide goes out and over she rolls."

"From what I read today in the library, this is the sort of spot that put Flynn's sailboat aground during a storm."

The boat driver overhears their conversation and nods his head in agreement. "Yes sir, mon. Da mista Flynn get his boat stuck on his first visit in da bad weather."

The chartered boat cruises slowly around the island, and they gaze at the shallow bottom and white sand beaches. Jon peers down through the clear tropical waters, and wipes the perspiration from his forehead. "We won't have any use for the scuba gear at this depth."

Chaz moves to the stern of the rolling boat deck and grabs up a mask and snorkel. "Hey Desmond, let's hold it here awhile, so we can go for a swim and check things out." The engines cut, and the boat drifts soundlessly on the undulating waves. Both Jon and Chaz strip their shirts and pull on swim fins. The military man, holding his mask tight to his face with the snorkel dangling at the side, is the first to tumble over the side. Jon looks around at the blue skies above and the green ocean below, before plopping backwards over the side into the warm, salty waters.

~*~

A pair of fluorescent green flip-flops shuffles along the crowded pier at the Key West Marina. Casey Kettles quietly whistles a tune to himself, as he approaches slip number nineteen, where Carlos keeps his ocean-going headquarters. The big henchman, Jorge, steps out from behind one of the tourist shacks and grabs Casey by the shirt collar.

The teenager squirms slightly, as the oversized gorilla lifts him off the ground. "Easy there, you big ape…"

Jorge heaves a grunt. "Carlos wants to talk with you." Casey tries to unclench the big man's grip, looks up at Jorge over his yellow-rimmed sunglasses and snidely replies,

"That's why I'm here, stupid." The large man releases the boy's shirt collar and gestures toward the waiting yacht.

Casey glances over his shoulder at the henchman and adjusts the stretched-out neck of his polo shirt. "I sure wonder why you don't have any other friends than Carlos..."

"Why?"

The boy looks up at the comparably tiny cranium perched between a pair of big shoulders. "Forget about it." Casey continues on to the yacht, and Jorge follows after him.

~*~

Water splashes, as Jon and Chaz both climb aboard the fishing boat with their snorkeling gear in hand. The Navy SEAL tosses his fins and mask near the scuba tanks and wipes the water from his short-cropped hair and beard. "Eh, Jon... You see anything down there?"

Jon puts a towel to his face and sweeps it back over his wet head. "Nope. Just sandy bottom, coral, and sea shells..."

In the shade of the main cabin, Desmond sits at the wheel of the boat, watching it turn with the movement of the waves. "What you be lookin' for out der?"

The pair looks to their driver, and they seem somewhat tentative to answer. Jon exchanges a glance with Chaz, and he shrugs as if to agree on them revealing their secret mission. Jon replies, "Can we trust you not to repeat anything?"

Desmond stands up straight, snaps a salute and smiles. "Yes, mon! I is the loyalist of dem driver-mons on the island. You say no-speak-it and dey surely not hear it from me."

Chaz grins, as Jon wipes the towel across his chest and continues. "I have a lady-friend that came here on research business a few weeks ago, and she thinks there might be some sort of treasure around."

The boat driver maintains his beaming smile and nods. "She be lookin' for Errol Flynn's treasure?"

Surprised, Chaz looks at Jon and then to Desmond. "You know something of it?"

"Ya, mon. Everybody in da island knows 'bout 'im. Dat's why dey named dis marina after 'im."

Astonished that the assumed secret was no secret after all, Jon utters, "So, everyone knows about it?"

"Ya, mon. Da Hollywood-man talk a lot about finding pirate booty around the island. Had big parties and kept his found treasures out 'ere in underwater caves."

Chaz tilts his head and raises his brow questioningly. "Do you know where the caves are?"

"No, mon. If I did, you would be seeing me in one of dos big yacht boats and not dis fishing tub."

Jon's ears perk up at the rumble of an airplane in the distance. He looks all around and then to the horizon and instantly recognizes the distinct sound of dual radial engines. "Hear that sound? It's very familiar…"

Chaz and Jon look to the sky northward and see the faint outline of a high-winged, flying boat coming their way. The military man scans their diving equipment on the deck and nudges Jon's backpack under the bench seat to conceal it. He shields the sunshine from his eyes and watches the low-flying airplane's silhouetted approach. "Whoever that is… They seem to be coming right this way."

Chaz grabs his bag and opens it to retrieve his gun, when Jon puts his hand out to stop him. "Wait a minute… That's the seaplane pilot you met at the Conch Republic."

"You're kidding me?"

Keeping his gun hand buried inside the duffle bag, Chaz stares out to the horizon as the seaplane flies nearer, barely skimming over the waves of the tranquil ocean waters. It finally touches down with a series of splashes and races toward the chartered fishing vessel like a winged speedboat.

All three on the ship deck watch in awe as the seaplane stays on the step, shooting water aside, cruising across the ocean surface toward the idle fishing boat.

As it nears the floating vessel, the large radial engines reduce power, and the seaplane settles lower in the water. Pulling up alongside the boat, the winged watercraft cuts the engines and bobs quietly alongside. The port-side, front window slides back and a head and arm stretch out from the pilot's seated position. The surprised, smiling mug of Rollie McKinny offers a salute as he greets them. "Ahoy-matey… Enjoying your vacation?"

XIX

The Key West Marina is filled with various hired boats, coming and going, with tourist-sightseers and sport fisherman. The luxury Cuban yacht, *Anastasia,* pulls out from the harbor and circles the island to the west, making its way around Mallory Square and the cruise ships. The midday sun glistens on the shiny yacht, as it cruises slowly past the pier, then powers up and points the bow due south.

~*~

Off the northern shore of Navy Island, the nose of the seaplane is tethered by a line to the stern of the fishing boat. Both watercrafts float independently a short distance from each other, as they undulate on the rolling waves. On the rear deck of the boat, everyone assembles. Chaz looks at Jon and grins knowingly. "See, I told you she'd find us."

Jon smirks with a joking retort. "Yep, you sure know women better than I do."

Chaz shrugs and snuffles his nose. "Well, I just know about finding people."

Elizabeth gives Jon a warm embrace and smiles at him. "I'm so glad to find you safe."

Rollie hops over to the boat deck from the nose hatch on the seaplane and shakes his head. "Jon, it seems like you drift further out to sea each time I catch up with you."

Jon holds Elizabeth and grips Rollie's hand to shake. His gaze returns to her, and he can't seem to believe his eyes. "After seeing your ransacked residence, I'm glad to know you're okay, too."

Elizabeth looks to Chaz, and he extends his hand. "Hello, I'm Chaz Treadwill."

She takes his hand and gives a friendly handshake. "I'm Elizabeth, an old friend." Glancing to Jon, she smiles. "I'm so sorry that Jon has mixed you up with all of this."

Chaz grins at the visitors and then looks to the plane. "It's always an adventure with Jon and any friends of his."

The happy reunion is disrupted, when Aston pokes his head from the hatch of the seaplane and calls over, "Hello der, writer-mon. Have you found any of dat treasure yet?"

Everyone on the ship deck turns to the bearded, buccaneer-styled islander standing up, waist-level, out from the seaplane's nose. Jon turns to look at Rollie questioningly. "Who else did you bring along with you?"

The pilot innocently looks around. "Aston is like the Jamaican James Bond. He spent a lot of time here in the seventies, so we figured he would be helpful in finding you."

Elizabeth squeezes Jon's hand. "Actually, it was because of having him along that we found you so quickly."

Jon turns to her. "Why's that?"

Rollie snorts his reply. "That Key Wester doesn't have a valid passport anymore."

Aston climbs out from the seaplane nose hatch and leaps to the stern of the bobbing fishing boat. "It is probably somewhere down here, stuck in Jamaica still. Dey never gave it back, when dey kicked me out."

Bewildered by all this, Jon asks, "How did you get back into the United States before?"

Aston smiles and winks broadly at Jon. "More or less, da same route as many Cuban refugees use to get dere."

Rollie pats Aston on the shoulder and looks to his seaplane. "Oh, yeah, that reminds me… I need to stop at Customs and refuel this water-bird, but I can't have any illegal passengers aboard."

Chaz looks over the side at the shallow, sandy bottom of the ocean and back at the pilot. "You could leave your passengers with us and meet us back here this afternoon."

The pilot looks at the pair that came along with him. "That okay with you both? Should only be a few hours…"

Elizabeth holds onto Jon's hand and nods her consent. "Yes. I'm sure we'll be entertained with plenty of adventure stories until your return." Rollie takes the boat's tether line, pulls it closer to the seaplane and then steps over to the nose. He climbs into the hatch and ducks down inside.

Standing at the fishing boat's stern, Aston gazes from the watery horizon to the shoreline of the nearby island. "Wow… Still look da same as before, after all des years."

From the shade of the boat cabin, Desmond comes out to the rear deck and stares strangely at the bearded islander who gazes longingly toward Navy Island. "Hallo, der mon. You have been to des waters before?"

At the sound of the thick Jamaican accent, Aston hops down from his perch and replies, "Yes, mon. Spent a lot of time on dis island. You live here longtime?"

Desmond flashes his pearly whites. "All my life I live here. What is it you call yerself?"

The Key Wester hesitates for a moment, while he has a look at the local Jamaican. "Aston... And what is yours?"

Desmond's eyes brighten with a burst of excitement at the recollection of the familiar name. "Wow, da mista Aston! My name is Desmond Clarke from da Ocho Rios."

Aston cocks a grin and strokes his beard thoughtfully. "Do you know a Jimmy Clarke from dose parts?"

Awestruck, the Jamaican answers. "Dat is my Fadda! But, I hear most of da funky stories of Aston, da wild 'nd crazy American-mon, from my sweet Mudda many a time!" Beneath his long whiskers, Aston appears to blush at the keen admiration of the local youth.

From the seaplane nose hatch, Rollie pops up and tosses Elizabeth's travel bag toward the deck. "Hey, Aston... Catch this! It's better that I don't have any unaccounted for luggage or contraband aboard in case the locals want to inspect my airplane." The pilot tosses off the boat's tether line and swings the hatch cover over. "Hope you all have a happy family reunion while I'm gone." Before it closes, he calls out to those aboard the fishing vessel. "I'll fly back around to pick you guys up in a few hours. Stay out of trouble!"

Aston hands Elizabeth her bag, as the seaplane drifts and then starts its engines. The Key West islander goes over to shake hands with Desmond and hugs him on the shoulder. "Has been awhile since I dove in dese warm Jamaican waters. Can you take us to da reef?"

Desmond grins, bobbing his head agreeably. "Yes, mon. Dems pretty waters o'er dere."

Aston nods. "And some caves."

Stepping away from Elizabeth, Jon perks up at Aston's mention of the reef. "Underwater caves?"

Elizabeth looks to Aston. "What caves?" He juts a boney finger toward her luggage bag and crinkles his brow. "Dat is where da skull come from and will lead us back to."

Jon and Chaz look to each other curiously, and the military man asks aloud, "And what skull is that?"

Elizabeth turns to them both, and Jon meets her gaze with a tilting of his head. "Yeah… What skull?"

~*~

Not far from Navy Island, around the bend of the shoreline and concealed from the fishing boat, a larger yacht waits as the seaplane taxies across the water and takes off. With binoculars, two of the darkly-dressed Jamaican thugs stand on the deck watching, as the fishing boat starts to motor away and the flying boat soars into the blue skies. One of the gang members nods his head toward the panel of tinted windows behind him and motions to follow after the boat.

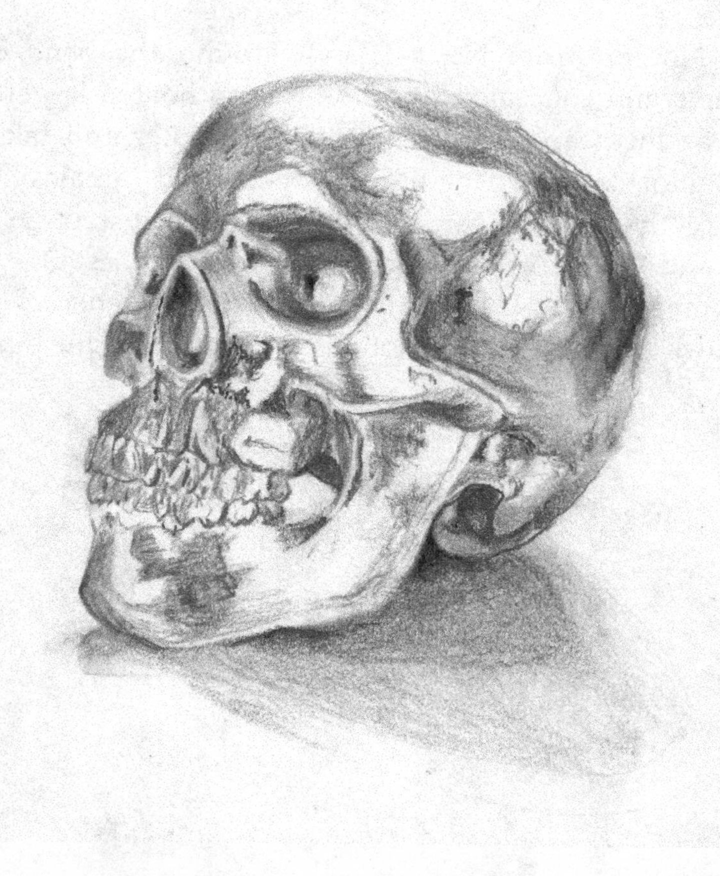

XX

The chartered fishing boat bobs and sways on the ocean surface several miles out from the shoreline of Navy Island. Jon and Elizabeth remain on deck with Desmond, perched at the side rail, watching down into the cloudy, blue depths. There is a dive flag buoy floating in the water not far off from the starboard bow.

Standing side by side at the rail, Elizabeth glances over at Jon, and he notices how her eyes sparkle with excitement. She grins at him sincerely and states. "I can't imagine what sort of escapades you've been on since living in the Keys."

Feeling a bit unsure about how to react to her awe, he puts on an expression of false modesty and smiles back at her. "Oh, you know... Pirates and adventures on the high seas... The usual kinda stuff."

She smiles at him like he's teasing. "And now I drag you down to Jamaica for a treasure hunt?"

"I wasn't getting much of my writing done anyway."

"How is it going? Is there a new book in the works?"

"Still trying to settle into a routine."

Elizabeth looks over to the golden skull nested on her opened backpack and sighs. "I should just be delighted with what I have found already."

Glancing over at the intriguing treasure, Jon shrugs. "Where did you actually find it?"

"I was snorkeling around the shoreline near to the same spot where we found you all, and a bit of the gold was shining through the sand. I dove down for a closer look and uncovered it."

Jon gazes back at Elizabeth and nods supportively. "And you think it is a part of a larger treasure find?"

She smiles and leans back to enjoy the warming sun. "The legend tells that the Hollywood actor, Errol Flynn, first came down here in the late nineteen-forties with his 118 foot schooner, Zaca." As she relates the story from memory, Jon is completely riveted. "During a tropical storm, he was forced to put in at Kingston, and then he made his way to Port Antonio. He declared it more beautiful than any woman he ever met."

Jon tilts his head and grins slyly. "So he hadn't met any Blackwright women?"

Amused, she swats at his hand, and continues with her story. "Anyway, Mister Flynn was a bit of an adventurer on and off the screen, so when he heard the local lore about treasure to be found in the waters around the island, he spent a lot of his time here hunting for it. "

"And I guess he found some?"

"Some say he did… And there are some who say he didn't. His movie career was on the decline, and he started to owe people a lot of money. He had already gone through several marriages, so he started spending his time in Jamaica. Eventually, he bought into the luxurious Titchfield Hotel off the peninsula, a local cattle farm, and Navy Island there, where he hosted parties for his celebrity friends."

Jon casts his gaze to the horizon, where the shores of the island can be faintly seen. "He bought an empty island?"

She delights in Jon's attention to her treasure tale and puts on her charming smile. "Well, the legend is that he won it in a rum-fueled poker game. There was nothing on it, but he stayed on his sailing yacht off the coast of the island instead of being docked in the port. There are some sources that believe he was secretly hiding the treasures he found in the former pirate waters surrounding Jamaica."

Concerned, Jon lowers his voice. "Like those men who ransacked your place in Oracabessa?"

Elizabeth nods. "There are people who are fanatically loyal to this island and its history… who think that any sort of tourism is merely selling out the soul of their country."

"What about treasure hunting?"

"They are wholeheartedly against any sort of artifact recovery, too." Elizabeth gazes off to the coast of Navy Island on the horizon with the faint shoreline of Jamaica behind it. "The Port Antonio marina is named after Flynn, but some locals still believe him to be the patron saint of tourist looters. He had quite the mixed reputation during his time here."

"From what I've read of him, he always has had a mixed reputation. It's tough having a Gemini personality and living two separate lifestyles while always in the public eye."

She turns to face her old friend and smiles knowingly. "You should know better than most, Mister *J. T. Springs*."

Desmond comes around to the stern from the bow of the fishing boat and smiles at the pair of reuniting friends. "Look-see dar. Dey come up now."

Elizabeth and Jon look over the side of the boat and observe, as a series of bubbles from the divers comes up alongside the fishing vessel. Chaz surfaces first, removing his mask and breathing regulator as he swims toward the boat. Not far behind, Aston comes to the surface and shakes his long hair and beard like a shaggy, wet sea-dog.

Desmond leans over the railing and pulls up Chaz's diving gear. Jon peers over the side and calls out to them. "Did you find anything down there?"

Chaz, with a particularly engaged expression on his face, continues to swim alongside while removing his fins. "We found some caves, but visibility is low right now with the sand washing in and out." He tosses his swim fins aboard and climbs over the side onto the deck, where Desmond hands him a towel. He takes a seat on the bench opposite Jon and Elizabeth, and flashes a grin. With a swift flick of his wrist, Chaz opens his palm to suddenly reveal a Spanish doubloon. The ancient coin shimmers in the sunlight, and Elizabeth and Jon are awestruck. Elizabeth blinks from her engaged stare and looks up at Chaz. "That was down there?"

"There is probably a whole lot more in those caves, but the sand is shifting through there too much, making it hard to find anything right now." The military man flips the gold coin through the air to Jon, so that he can make a closer examination. "I just got lucky and found that one, when I sifted my fingers through the sandy bottom of the cave."

Helping Aston make his way over the side rail, Desmond looks back at the group examining the old coin. "Dem doubloons occasionally wash up on da beach in town and keep da legends fresh."

Aston stands on the deck shaking himself off. With his beard and shaggy mop of hair, the lean islander in his slim-cut swimsuit looks like a wet cue-tip. Looking out at the surrounding blue waters of the Caribbean, Aston pats

Desmond on the shoulder and smiles. "Yes, mon, a bit o' gold will keep da whispers on da lips."

Chaz dries himself with a towel and turns to Aston. "Did you find anything down there?"

Aston replies, grinning. "Ahh, da piece of mind."

Jon turns to study the Spanish doubloon in his hand and then looks to the sopping-wet islander. "Anything else?" Aston shrugs at Jon and then looks to the rest of the crew. "Not on dis here visit, but I have found items in da past."

Fascinated, Jon stares at the former Jamaican explorer. "Was it pirate treasure?"

Aston grins slyly and slowly looks around at each of their attentive faces. He gestures to the gold and remarks, "Dem is stashed goodies from da greatest of all da movie swashbucklers… Mista Flynn. Ya know, I don't smoke da dope, so why else would I be kicked outta Jamaica for good?"

Elizabeth pipes in and nods her head in agreement. "Funding your stay with treasure would upset some locals."

Aston smiles and winks at her. "Made me unpopular with da some, but very popular with many of da others."

Desmond chimes in. "Some of dem is the da stories I heard from my Mudda!" The Key Wester bashfully squeezes ocean water from his long beard and takes up a towel to dry off. "Yes, I only told yer family da good stories."

Chaz nods to the diving gear and makes a suggestion to Jon. "Hey, buddy! There's still another hour on those air tanks, if you both want to take a look-see."

The dry pair exchange a look of excitement, and then Jon nods in agreement. "Looks like fun. Since we're already here, we might as well take a look to see what we can find." He puts his arm on Elizabeth's shoulder and ushers her toward the diving gear. "I think we have enough time before our flight home arrives."

XXI

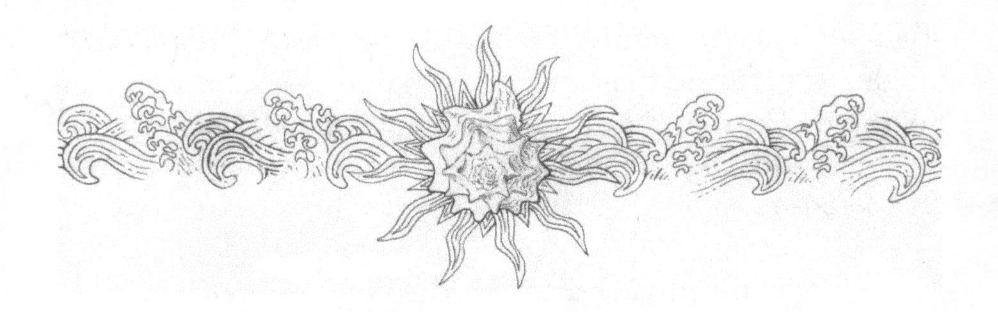

The Key West Air Charters seaplane sits at a small airstrip near Ocho Rios, Jamaica. Ian Fleming International Airport consists of just a single runway with a few small hangars and a shed-style building where a Customs employee occasionally makes his visits. The amphibious, twin engine aircraft sits along the landing strip beside a small private jet and a turboprop Caravan.

Stepping into the tropical heat, Rollie exits the rear door of the main building while talking to an airport worker. The pilot holds a half-eaten sandwich in one hand and a scratched-up, recycled bottle of Coke in the other. He groans. "Yes, I do understand all that, but what I want to know is this: Has the fuel truck arrived yet?"

"No, mon. Be here today or maybe tomorrow."

Walking alongside the unhelpful employee as he heads toward the parking lot, Rollie slows his step, shaking his head. "Wait a minute! Nobody said anything earlier about it possibly coming in tomorrow…"

The worker shrugs and continues to amble along. "Things mostly happen on da island time down here, Mista. Today could mean tomorrow, or da next day, who knows?"

Frustrated and defeated, Rollie returns to the shade of the building and sits on a rusty lawn chair facing the runway. He gazes across the single paved strip to the three different styles of aircraft parked on the grassy lawn fronting the jungled terrain. He finishes the last bite of his sandwich and takes a drink from the scuffed-up bottle of soda. Relaxing to doze in the creaky old chair, he murmurs quietly to himself, "Its island-time, Mon… Maybe tomorrow, maybe next day…"

~*~

Jon, with a diving mask perched on his forehead, pulls on the shoulder straps of the single air tank. From the cabin quarters below deck, Elizabeth comes out wearing a yellow swim top and slim cut bikini bottoms that ride low and straight across her hips. Remarkably fit and athletic for a middle-aged woman, she struts across the boat deck. "Jonathan… Don't go diving off without me and leave me behind to find you again. "

Jon turns toward her and can't help but notice her revealing swim outfit. He grins, as he adjusts the straps of the diving tank on his shoulders and responds to her humorously. "I'll be glad to follow along behind you." Chaz lifts a telling eyebrow and watches, as she bends over the pile of gear to grab a mask. Aston whistles softly, pushing his hair back. "Why'd I get 'ta partner wit da fella, 'nd not da lady?"

Elizabeth takes a seat on the port side of the stern, while Desmond helps her to fit the scuba tank on her back. Beside her, Jon waits until she is ready, and they both drop backward over the side into the clear, blue, tropical waters.

~*~

The sunlight from above shimmers through the waves and casts the boat in a distorted underwater image. Jon swims beside Elizabeth, as they descend toward the coral reef. Schools of colorful fish laze and then suddenly dart past them, as the two casually swim through the topography on the ocean floor. After searching along the sandy bottom awhile, they finally arrive at what looks to be a small opening to a cave beneath a coral shelf.

Through diving masks and cloudy water, Jon and Elizabeth's gazes meet. With excited trepidation, she reaches out for Jon's hand and gives it a loving squeeze. Bubbles roll up from Jon's breathing apparatus as he ushers her ahead with a gentlemanly gesture.

Elizabeth nods and kicks her fins forward, swimming through the small opening with a trailing swish of sand. Jon, eyes wide with excitement, follows her under the ledge and into the coral cave.

~*~

Topside, the ocean waves are beginning to roll a bit more aggressively, as the divers finally come to the surface. Jon pushes his diving mask up to his forehead, spits the breathing regulator from his mouth and looks curiously at an unknown ocean yacht tied opposite their rented fishing boat. He turns to find Elizabeth beside him, and, when he turns back toward the fishing boat, he is greeted by a dark-skinned thug pointing a cocked hunting rifle directly at them.

Treading water, Jon raises his hands up high and glances at Elizabeth. "Are these the sorts of bad men you were telling me about?"

She bobs in the water alongside Jon, spits out her regulator, and wipes the strands of wet hair from her face. "Yes… They are exactly what I was talking about."

At the stern of the boat, another Jamaican thug holding a cocked handgun points it and beckons them to come aboard. Elizabeth looks to Jon and murmurs, "I'm so sorry about this."

Jon gulps, as he looks up at the armed man's familiar features. A cold feeling of dread washes over him, as he stares at the white bandage stretched across the bridge of the man's broken nose. He replies timidly, "Yeah… Me, too."

XXII

Floating at the surface of the rolling waves, Jon watches as Elizabeth is quickly pulled aboard the chartered watercraft. He swims over and climbs on deck to be greeted by the dour faces of the Jamaican thugs. Seated in the cabin below, Desmond and Aston sit quietly, as another thug points a machine gun at them. Jon's eyes dart across the boat deck, searching for Chaz, hoping for the best, but fearing the worst.

The Jamaican thug shoves Jon over next to Elizabeth, and the other thug keeps the rifle pointed in their direction. He growls at them and prods Jon with the end of the pistol. "Give us what you find down dere."

Jon opens both of his hands to reveal empty palms. "Find? We are just here on our vacation."

"We know who you are and why you be here!"

Trying to diffuse the mounting tension and draw away the guns pointed at Lizzy, Jon protests. "I'm just a writer..."

The thug backhands Jon across the mouth, raises his firearm and growls vehemently. "Not you, Mista... Her!"

The two thugs glare at Elizabeth, who clutches something small in her hand. "What do you have dere?"

Elizabeth opens her hand to reveal a miniature carved figure that looks to be crafted of aged ivory. The thug leans closer and grumbles "What is dat?"

She shrugs and holds it out to him. "I thought it was a piece of driftwood."

The Jamaican eagerly snatches the small carved piece from her hand and passes it over to the man with the rifle. "Take dat to da boat and show it to Jamal." The thug holds the personal note, addressed to Jon from Elizabeth, and takes out the treasure map from the envelope. He examines the folded piece of paper and turns it over to examine the blank backside. He scowls, unimpressed, and tosses the map aside. "Dis 'ere is nutting but fake tourist trash." He looks to the other man again and barks, "Take dat carved t'ing to 'im 'nd ask what we are to do wit dem?"

The man with the rifle hands the long gun over to the other thug and pulls a tether-line to bring the two boats closer. He leaps aboard the yacht, and the other gangster ushers Jon and Elizabeth down to the lower cabin area to join the others. He growls at the attending guard. "Watch dem all until Sammy gets back."

Leaving the four hostages with the sentry, Jon watches as the thug returns to the stern of the smaller boat. He leans over to Elizabeth. "What do you think they'll do?"

Melancholic, she stares forward and quietly responds. "If they're officially a part of the Jamaican Booty Posse, they'll murder us and burn the boat."

As Jon goes pale at the mention of their possible fate, Aston adds with a whisper, "Or worse…"

Jon turns to Aston. "What could be worse?"

The sentry with the gun pokes it at Jon and grumbles. "Quiet now. No talk from you dere!" Jon acquiesces with a nod and looks around for Chaz, who is nowhere to be seen. The guard moves up a step toward the rear of the boat and watches two men converse on the bow of the larger yacht.

An argumentative commotion is heard from the other vessel, and everyone attempts to overhear the muted voices. Elizabeth, being nearest to them, tries to listen. "I can't understand them very well."

Seated the furthest away, Desmond stares ahead and speaks quietly. "Dey arguing about what to do wit us, and who dere might be ta come lookin' after we's found missin'."

Elizabeth leans forward and looks down the line of hostages to the driver. "Who *would* come looking?"

Desmond shrugs and gravely stares forward. "Dey saw us earlier wit da pilot-man in da flying boat-plane and tink he might come back."

Jon looks at his empty wrist where his watch was. "Yeah, Rollie should be coming back around anytime."

Aston shakes his head and responds discouragingly. "Da Rollie-mon knows better than to put down in foreign waters wit an unfamiliar boat bein' around."

Jon seems surprised. "What? He landed earlier."

"Dat was to drop me at a fish-boat. Some US dollars easy to buy off a poor fisherman, but not a big, fancy yacht."

Elizabeth curiously looks around, and just now notices that one of them is missing. "Jon, where is your Navy friend?"

Aston combs his fingers through his scraggly beard and quietly replies. "Da Navy-mon slips o'er da side when we were approached. He say, it better to be safe than sorry."

Relieved, Jon nods his agreement. "Sounds like him. He's always been funny like that, ever since being escorted from the Hollywood sign by the LA police helicopter."

Interested, Elizabeth glances at Jon. "I didn't think anyone was permitted to hike up there…"

"That's what the LAPD, County Park Rangers and the appointed judge all told us, too."

She crinkles her brow. "Where is he now?"

Aston rolls his eyes down and gestures to the boat's floorboards. Jon picks up on the hint and softly whispers, "He's down under the deck?"

Aston appears a bit uncertain, and responds. "We think he's under da boat..."

Up near the cabin opening, the Jamaican thug with the rifle looks back at the prisoners to silence them. He then peers back toward the other boat and continues listening to the lively argument.

Aboard the yacht, the two quarrelling Jamaicans move it inside, but their angry voices can still be heard in muted tones as the door slams closed. The pair of armed thugs on the fishing boat moves closer astern, attempting to listen while the floating vessels slowly drift farther apart. One of the Jamaicans finally notices the increased distance and reaches over the side to gather up the tether line. He pulls it in until the cut-end of the marine rope hangs limp in his hand.

He leans out to peek over the side rail, and the sharp crack of a pistol shot echoes across the surface of the water. Alerted, the thug with the rifle raises it to his shoulder, pointing it out to sea, and looks back quickly at the hostages. The Jamaican leaning over the side of the boat slumps down and tumbles overboard with a bullet wound to his forehead. The remaining gangster turns to point his rifle at the hostages and another snapping set of gunshots breaks the brief silence. The thug with the rifle pitches forward with two consecutive bullet hits placed center-mass and another one to his temple. A spray of blood mists through the air near the cabin entry.

The dead man crumples, revealing where the bullets passed through the body to bury themselves in the wooden trim.

Aston instantly jumps to his feet and rushes to the controls of the fishing boat. He waves a finger at Desmond and points him toward the front of the watercraft. "Make sure all dem tether lines are free!" The Jamaican driver climbs through the forward window to the bow, and Aston looks back as Jon pulls Elizabeth to her feet.

At the stern, the wet Navy SEAL, with marine engine grease painted across his features, climbs up with a pistol in hand. The waterproof duffle secured across his back sheds drips of water. With a water-soaked thud, Chaz leaps to the boat deck and rushes toward Jon and Elizabeth in the cabin. He calls out to Aston at the controls and waves forward. "We're good to go, so let's get!"

The fishing boat's dual engines quickly rumble to life below the deck, and Aston pushes both throttles full forward. As the fishing boat cuts through the water, leaving one floating body behind, Jon and Chaz toss the other dead gangster overboard into the churned, v-shaped wake. Relieved, Jon looks to his friend. "Thanks, pal… I thought we were all going to die."

The military man grins and smears away some of the engine grease from his cheek. "Failure is not an option."

From around the cabin, Desmond, wide-eyed with shock, appears at the stern. He points to the large yacht behind them, and shakes his head in dismay. "I don't mean to be da sour apple in da barrel, but dat bigga boat will have no problem ta catch us, right quick!"

Chaz winks at Desmond and replies, "No worries. While underwater, I tied a length of that tether line around their props. It will be a real tight mess when they start up their engines and should hold them awhile." Everyone looks at the yacht as it starts its engines, pushes forward a short distance, then stalls out and turns to idle in the waves.

Behind the boat controls, Aston strokes his beard in contemplation. "I don't think it be safe to return to Port-A if dem fellas have a marine radio 'nd oth'a friends."

Chaz clicks his handgun's safety on and tucks it away. "I would assume they do. Where else can we get ashore?"

As the fishing boat races along through the waves, Desmond makes his way to Aston. "I know a place, just to da east of Port Antonio, where we can hideout."

The Key Wester looks at Desmond and smiles. "Frenchman's Cove?"

Desmond grins widely in return. "You been der?"

"I courted many a fine lady-friend on dat peaceful strip of sandy beach." Aston graciously steps away from the ship wheel, motioning Desmond to take command. "It's yer boat, Mista Captain."

XXIII

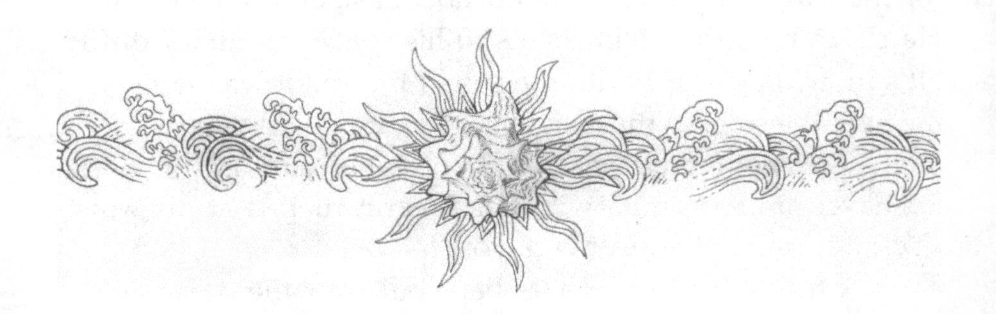

The fishing boat cruises at full speed through choppy water, as the jungle shores of Jamaica pass by in the distance. The small boat pounds the ocean and bounces across waves at a jarring pace, until Desmond finally eases back the throttles and slows the vessel. Pointing to a narrow strip of beach in a secluded inlet, Desmond comments, “Der she is… Frenchman’s Cove.”

The boat slowly turns toward the overgrown shoreline, while Elizabeth gazes out to the open waters just behind them. Jon stands next to her, puts his arm around her shoulders and pulls her close. "Are you okay?"

“I’m having a real hard time believing that those men were just killed back there.”

Jon nods thoughtfully and takes a measured breath before speaking. “Yes, I know… And it was about to be us.”

She turns and buries her face in Jon’s shoulder for comfort. “I’m sorry for getting you into this. It’s just that most of the murder and killing in my research usually happens hundreds of years before I come along to find the artifacts." She suddenly lifts her head from Jon's chest and turns to see her open backpack spilled out on the deck boards of the boat. "What happened to the treasure skull?"

Standing at the ship railing, Chaz, keeping a lookout for the gangster yacht, hears Elizabeth ask about the treasure. He clears his throat and points to his soaked, military duffle. "It's in my bag along with the coin. I figured it was safer with me over the side, so those men didn't catch sight of it."

Elizabeth breathes a sigh of relief and looks to the unshaven military man with the firearm tucked at his waist. "Yes, it is probably safest with you."

Chaz shrugs and gazes back out over the ocean again. "I don't know about that… People tend to shoot at the guy with the gun."

Jon tries to stay calm while processing their situation. "If Rollie can find our position to pick us up, maybe we can avoid them altogether and stay clear of anymore shooting."

The boat pulls through the narrow entrance to the cove, and Chaz leaps to the deck near where Aston is relaxing with his eyes shut. He looks to Desmond at the ship wheel and shakes his head. "We won't be able to raise him on the marine radio without calling out our own position."

Jon grunts, "Is that the bad news?"

The soldier looks to the fuel gauge on the boat and sighs. "Not really." Frowning, he turns to his companions. "We don't have enough fuel to keep running, and hiding in this cove might have us backed into a corner."

Elizabeth looks out to the peaceful, sandy shoreline. "What are we going to do?"

Standing beside her, Jon, trying to remain calm, replies, "Not much we can do… "

Chaz cheerfully chimes in. "Just like in the field... Hope and wait for the right opportunity."

~*~

At the Ian Fleming International Airport, under the shade of a palm tree, slumped in the rusty old chair, Rollie sleeps with his head canted to an odd angle, snoring quietly. The three airplanes still sit across the runway. A spindly cow with a washboard ribcage calmly ambles along, chewing its cud near scattered tufts of grass at the edge of the tree line. The only sounds are the crisp snap of the wind sock at the end of the runway and the occasional buzz of a mosquito.

~*~

The fishing boat motors into Frenchman's Cove and pulls nearer to the white-sand beach. Desmond spins the ship wheel to turn the boat, facing it out toward open water again. They all gather their belongings together, unsure if this is the location that they will depart from. Elizabeth gazes at the protected waters of the cove and the beach hemmed in by jungle. "It really is a beautiful place..."

Chaz grunts under his breath, as he reloads the clip on his handgun. "And a good place to die..."

She glances over her shoulder at him and grimaces. "That was not how I was going to finish my sentence."

Slapping in the fresh ammo clip, Chaz tucks his firearm in a pocket on his duffle bag and swings it over his shoulder. "In my sort of business, that's sometimes all we can hope for. Let's go ashore and get the lay of the land, before its dark."

Jon looks to Elizabeth, then to Chaz and the others. "Should we all go?"

Standing on the ship rail at the stern, Aston spreads his arms out wide. His clothes are tied in a bundle and hung across his shoulder like a sling. "See y'all on da beach..."

Aston dives overboard, and Chaz watches him knife into the shallow water and then swim toward shore.

Looking away from the beach, Chaz comments to Jon. "How about you stay with her and our driver-pal on the boat, while Robinson Crusoe and I check to see if the coast is safe." Chaz arches a thumb over his shoulder toward Aston, as the islander making his way up the beach shakes his beard and wet mop of hair like a dog after a swim.

Jon looks to Elizabeth, and she nods her agreement. Scanning their surroundings, Jon asks. "Okay, but what is our game plan if they happen to find us before you get back?"

The Navy SEAL steps to the shore-side of the fishing boat and holds onto the shoulder straps of his duffle bag. "You still have the gun from the guy you punched out?"

"Uh… Yeah?"

"Then you should use it, if you need to." Chaz gives a thumbs-up and dives in with his pack, skimming just under the surface of the clear, water.

Elizabeth turns to face Jon with a look of astonishment. "Jonathan, you have a gun?"

He nods timidly and glances across the deck to his bag. "Yes, I guess I do."

"Did I hear that you punched someone out for it?"

Smiling apologetically, Jon looks to the mouth of the cove and shrugs. "He didn't give me much of a choice."

Elizabeth seems somewhat reproachful, as she stares at her longtime friend. "You're not becoming one of those violent characters you write about, are you?"

Rising from the cabin below, Desmond overhears their conversation and smiles. "You's a writer-mon?"

Jon welcomes the change of subject and turns to him. "Yeah, I write sometimes."

The Jamaican puffs his chest and smiles. "When I'm drivin' da folks around, I come up wit all kinds of story ideas. Some of dem I write down even. "

Jon nods his approval. "That's the key to being a writer. It's just getting the story down on paper…"

Desmond reaches his long, slender arms up to hang on the cabin roof edge and ruminates on his desired profession. "I thought I had dem good adventure ideas until I start to drive you 'nd your friends around. Now it feels like I'm in one of dem *J. T. Springs* novels."

Jon glimpses over at Elizabeth, and she rolls her eyes. The driver smiles at their entertained reaction, commenting, "You like to write some like 'im someday?"

"Yeah, something along those lines…"

Desmond smiles blissfully, as he holds the lip of the roof and swings backward. "Aww, dat's so cool, mon. Someday, I want to write about a Jamaican adventure-man like da James Bond." He drops from his hanging grip and assumes the gun-toting stance of the secret agent.

Jon and Elizabeth turn their attention to the shoreline, as Chaz and Aston disappear into the jungle. She smiles at her long-time friend, and they exchange a humorous moment. Elizabeth mutters softly, "All you need is a creative muse."

XXIV

Rollie walks along a rusty section of chain link fence that surrounds the island airport. Passing the time, he strolls to the end of the runway and approaches some old, abandoned structures at the edge of the airport grounds. He peeks inside one of the ramshackle buildings and sees piles of garbage and a pair of empty fuel canisters.

Moving into the cooling shade of the unused hangar, he walks over and taps each of the fuel jugs with his foot to hear an empty, metallic thud. He scans around at the apparent dumping ground for the airport with the random collection of scrapped junk. Stepping back out into the afternoon sun, he walks back toward the parked airplanes, murmuring under his breath. "No fuel today… maybe tomorrow."

~*~

With the last hours of daylight, the sky begins to color. The chartered fishing boat sits waiting in the cove, bobbing silently, positioned with the bow pointed out to open waters. When the two explorers break out from the jungle, and onto the beach, Aston sits in the sand like a shipwrecked sailor. From the boat, Jon and Elizabeth observe, as Chaz sheds his duffle, makes his way into the water and swims toward them. They wait until he pulls himself aboard before Jon inquires, "So, what are our prospects?"

Chaz looks at his timepiece a moment, while he catches his breath following the swim. "Well, here's how it stands..." His gaze travels over to the gear piled on the deck. "We have a boat with barely enough fuel to make it back to Port Antonio, a few weapons aboard to defend ourselves and some diving gear with nearly empty tanks."

Elizabeth raises her hand and tries to cheerfully add, "And a working radio."

Chaz nods with agreement, and turns to Desmond. "Yeah, I thought more about that, but whatever we put out there on the radio airwaves, they will most likely be picking up before your pilot-friend does. "

Jon sighs and looks to Aston on the beach. "Did you come up with any sort of plan for escape, or was this just a check-list of the great things we have going for us?"

Amused by Jon's sarcasm, Chaz chuckles and turns toward the sight of Aston kicking out his feet on the beach. "Your Key West pal, Aston there, thinks he can remember the way to a vacation resort nearby or, at least, to the main road. Chances are that we could possibly get a lift or borrow some sort of transportation."

Jon seems skeptical of following the eccentric islander, sunning himself on the beach. "What about the boat?"

Motioning Desmond closer, Chaz wipes the wet from his short-cropped beard and puts his other hand to the Jamaican's shoulder. "Desmond, do you think you could find your way back to Port Antonio in the dark?"

"Yeah, Mon. I could find my way home in da darkness. No problem for me."

"Good to hear. We will make our way by land, and you can slip out of here at nightfall." Pulling a wad of wet cash from his pants pocket, Chaz peels off several large bills and offers them to the boat driver. "Will this be okay to cover the rental and your trouble?"

Desmond hesitantly takes the offered money and smiles with appreciation. "Yes, Sir-Mon! Dat not a problem. When I get back to Portie, I come and get you wit da car?"

Chaz considers the option a moment and nods his agreement. "That would work out just fine."

Jon watches Chaz tuck his money away and wonders, "What about Rollie and our ride home?"

Chaz zips closed his secure pants pocket and replies, "Hopefully, he is already at Navy Island and waiting for us."

Seemingly concerned, Elizabeth puts out the question. "What about the men who are trying to kill us?"

Chaz looks to the beach and expanse of jungle beyond. "The plan is to be gone before they catch up to us."

~*~

The bright orb of sun slowly drops below the horizon. Rollie climbs in through the rear cargo door of the seaplane to settle in for the night. As the evening light dims, the pilot gets situated amidst the clanking sounds of shifting gear. Occasional chatter of island birds and the clicking of tropical insects fill the humid air.

~*~

Twilight has settled over Frenchman's Cove. Jon, Elizabeth and Chaz swim for shore, holding their belongings above the water while they swim. They make their way up onto the sandy shoreline to retrieve Chaz's duffle, and Aston opens his resting eyes to look at them. Moustache whiskers that overhang his lips curl up to reveal a smile, and the sleepy islander utters, "We's not been killed yet?"

Chaz picks up his bag by one of the shoulder straps. "Not yet… Are you ready to lead us out of here?"

Looking the image of a beached bum, Aston sits up and looks around, still not entirely awake from his snooze. "Maybe we can find us some bikes in dat resort near to here? Was havin' some pleasant dreams of ridin' my own chariot with da wind in my hair and my feathered friend on my arm."

Elizabeth adjusts the straps on her bag and remembers her first introduction to Aston outside the Clipped Kitty. Rubbing her chin, she gazes at the dark jungle foliage lining the isolated beach. "Stealing four bikes for us…? I'd rather we not have the Jamaican police after us, too."

Aston climbs to his feet, pats the sand from his bottom, looks around to get his bearings, and then points to the west. "Okay, this is da way for da jungle tour to da Port Antonio." He marches across the pristine beach with his sandals in hand, pauses a second and then turns around, rethinking his direction of travel.

Chaz watches and then motions them after Aston. "Don't worry about it. He has it figured out now… I think." The group starts to follow Aston into the thick undergrowth, as they hear the engines of their chartered vessel starting up. The rumbling sound of the departing craft slowly decreases as it makes its way out of the cove and into the darkness.

XXV

Back on the island of Key West, the Conch Republic Tavern is packed with Hemingway look-alikes of all shapes and sizes. The copious drinkers seem to be having a fine time, and the clamor in the saloon is well above conversation level, as tropical island music blasts through the house speaker system. The owner of the establishment scans around the room looking for someone and finds them at the end of the bar.

After serving another mixed drink across the counter, Angie makes her way down to the end of the slab where the chief mechanic for Key West Air Charters sits having a beer. She leans across the bar top and raises her voice to him. "Anything else I can get you, Ace?"

"Thanks, honey… I'm good."

"No word from Rollie yet?"

Ace takes a swig from his beer and shakes his head. "All I know is what he wrote on that scrap of paper for me."

"You think he took that woman to look for Springer?"

"He's done dumber stuff…"

Forcing a smile, Angie attempts to hide her concern. "Hey, have you seen Carlos around?"

Ace shakes his head, flummoxed, and looks to his beer. "All I've seen the last few days is Hemingway, Hemingway, and Hemingway."

She raps the bar top with her knuckles and looks to another waiting customer, a few white-bearded patrons down. "Let me know if you need anything else Ace, or if you hear from them."

"Sure thing, darlin'."

~*~

The night air is still warm, as the small group of travelers follows Aston through the dense island foliage. Elizabeth walks behind Jon, with Chaz cautiously at the rear. Aston stops and looks upward through the treetops to gage the position of the stars. Bathed in sweat, Jon approaches Aston and whispers, "You still know where you're going?"

Aston looks behind to the others, strokes his beard and grins through the dim light. "I's know where I'm goin'… Maybe not where you's goin'."

Jon mulls the peculiar response and gestures ahead. "How about we all stick together?"

Aston nods, pointing in the direction to their right. "Many tings do change a lot over da years, but some tings stay da same." He proceeds to walk on.

Elizabeth whispers in Jon's ear. "What does that mean? Is he completely lost?"

"I don't know."

Jon turns to gaze at Elizabeth and then to Chaz, who shrugs nonchalantly and replies, "Hey, if we don't know where we are, the people chasing us probably don't either."

Jon looks back to Elizabeth and remarks, "Somehow, I don't find that at all reassuring." He sees Aston disappear into the thick tangle of jungle and follows after him.

~*~

The tropical night is quiet, with the exception of the rattling hum of a window AC unit. The nighttime security lights from the main building of the international airport shine across the airstrip. A dark figure carries something toward the parked aircrafts and ducks into the concealing shadows, as the nighttime security guard walks outside to have a smoke.

Finishing his hand-rolled cigarette, the night-guard tosses the butt aside, looks around briefly, and then opens the door and steps back inside. From the shadows between the aircrafts, Rollie appears with the fuel canisters in hand and a coiled length of garden hose. He places the old, dented cans under the turboprop airplane and looks up to the fuel tanks on the high wings. "Sorry guys, but I have to be leaving in the morning…" Rollie jams a length of hose into the opening of the fuel canister and holds the other end, as he climbs onto the airplane wing.

~*~

After several hours of hiking, Aston finally leads the small group out of the jungle brush to a small, unlit roadway. At the edge of the vegetation, they see Aston orient himself with the stars again and then look each way down the empty roadway. Jon clears his throat and asks, "Which way now?"

Chaz motions over to the right. "I think that's North." With a nod, Aston gestures up the road and starts walking.

Unsure, Jon looks to Elizabeth and ushers her along. "Well, he got us this far at least."

She wipes the dripping perspiration from her temple. "Yeah, wherever this is…"

~*~

The chartered fishing boat slowly motors into the bay at Port Antonio on its way home to the Errol Flynn Marina. Desmond steps out to fasten the lines as the boat pulls alongside the dock, and two men in dark clothing emerge from the shadows to greet him. One of the armed thugs jumps into the boat. The other, on the dock, pulls Desmond aside. "Where you take dem to?"

Still holding the docking lines, Desmond raises his hands up high, shakes his head, and pleads his innocence. "Dey say I take dem, or dey kill me!"

The thug motions for him to put down his hands and looks around cautiously. The man in the boat climbs out to the dock and shakes his head at not finding anyone inside. "Where you let dem off?"

"Morant Bay. I hear dem say dey get first flight out of Kingston." The thug looks at Desmond suspiciously and then looks back at the other thug. Unsure, he checks his watch, calculates the timeframe and puts his gun away.

Desmond waits as the two men step aside on the dock and discuss the situation. The main thug moves back and shoves a slip of paper in the front pocket of Desmond's shirt. He puts a firm grip on the driver's shoulder and leans in close to tersely whisper. "You hear from dem, and you be sure to let us know, okay? Big reward for dem pillagers of our island."

Desmond nods his head in agreement and responds, "Yes, mon. I hear from dem, and you will know of it."

Satisfied with the boat driver's answer, the two thugs walk back down the pier and climb into their parked car. Desmond watches, as the imported Japanese vehicle's headlights flick on, the engine starts and the car drives away. He finishes securing the boat to the dock and looks around at the vacant pier. Finally, he climbs back aboard the vessel and begins to unload the diving gear.

~*~

Headlights appear on the quiet jungle road, and Aston quickly motions for them all to duck back behind the tree line. The car approaches slowly, scanning the roadside ditch and underbrush with flashlights, shining out from the rolled-down windows. Set back from the road, Elizabeth squats down low and whispers quietly to Jon, "Are those our Booty thugs?"

"I would assume so."

"If they're looking for us way out here, they probably have eyes searching the whole island."

Jon nods his head, as the automobile cruises slowly by. After the car headlights pass, Aston steps out onto the road, looks around and waves them all onward. Chaz steps from the bushes beside Jon and Elizabeth. He has his gun in hand but tucks it away after seeing that the roadway is clear. "That's not good, seeing them out here." He glances to Jon, readjusts the duffle pack on his shoulders and continues. "They definitely have the word out to hunt for us."

They watch Aston continue his carefree stroll down the dark roadway. Elizabeth takes a deep, calming breath and suggests to the two men beside her, "Maybe we could just give them what we found?"

Chaz shakes his head at her suggestion. "They would never believe that those are the only valuable items we found. We will be much better off using evade-and-escape tactics than risking direct contact."

Jon tries to comfort Elizabeth by putting his arm around her and giving a gentle squeeze. "I think Chaz is right. We just need to hide out a bit longer, until we can find Rollie.

They continue to follow Aston down the road, until another pair of headlights approaches through the darkness. Aston waves them aside, and everyone ducks into the jungle again as the car slowly nears. From behind palms and hanging tree vines, they observe as a Mercedes cruises past.

After the most recent drive-by clears their line of sight, they reconvene on the roadway to continue their journey. Chaz walks beside Jon and, in a hushed voice, speaks to him. "Did that last one look like our driver's car?"

Jon thinks a moment before nodding his agreement. "Yeah, it did. But whoever was behind the wheel was a whole lot shorter."

"I thought so too."

With bright stars lighting the path before them, Jon takes a look over his shoulder at the empty road behind them. He mutters to Chaz, "It appears that we have a long walk ahead of us."

Chaz flexes his shoulders back and quietly confides, "Yep, unless we can come up with something better."

Jon looks to his military friend and takes a slow, calming breath to steady his nerves. "Yeah… A plan would be great about now."

XXVI

On the eastern horizon, the morning sky begins to glow. Parked beside the single runway, across from the airport buildings, the aircrafts maintain the same positions they occupied the night before. Inside the Grumman seaplane, Rollie is at the controls going through his preflight checklist. He switches on each engine. The big radials fire up, and the propeller blades begin to rotate.

The high-winged seaplane slowly rolls forward and taxis toward the length of runway. At the end of the airstrip, the tail pivots around, and the aircraft points its nose down the tarmac. Holding in place with the wheel brakes engaged, the plane's dual engines release a belch of smoky exhaust and throttle up. Releasing the brakes, the seaplane quickly lunges forward, gains speed and gradually rises up into the air. Gaining altitude, the seaplane circles above the airport and tips its wing in a farewell salute. Rising higher into the sky, the flying boat soars toward open water and the morning sun.

~*~

Squatted down, hiding in the bushes again, the four fugitives wait, as another car motors slowly past their position. Chaz looks past Elizabeth to Jon and shakes his head. "This is getting ridiculous. We're coming on daybreak, and the road traffic will only be increasing. We have more than a few miles to Port Antonio. If we want to get there sometime today, we're going to need a new plan." He looks to their guide, who sits hugging his knees while stroking his beard. "Any ideas, Aston?"

"Dis road will take us dere, pretty sure. I could go on ahead 'nd bring us back some transportation."

Chaz thinks a moment, as he waits for the road to clear. "Or, we could just hijack something here…"

Jon grimaces and looks at his friend questioningly. "Hijack? That sounds risky…"

The Navy SEAL nods and stares out to the now empty road. "Taking calculated risks is what life is all about."

Following them out from the cover of the brush, Elizabeth looks down the road to where the last car has just disappeared around the turn. "What did you have in mind?"

Pivoting around to face Elizabeth, Chaz studies her tight blouse, long blonde hair and short-hemmed khaki shorts. "Hate to say it, but you're our best bet for attracting a ride."

Jon steps forward in protest. "No, it's too dangerous."

Chaz shakes his head and holds up a reassuring hand. "Wait a minute. All we need is someone to stop their vehicle. No one is going to pull over for Aston or me, with our faces, and you look too…"

Jon gets a peculiar look on his face. "Too, what…?"

The seasoned soldier scratches his beard and laughs. "Don't know what to call it… White-American looking."

"So?"

Chaz shrugs. "Nobody wants to help the pretty-dude."

Elizabeth steps forward and swoops back her hair. "What do I have to do?"

With a gesture, Chaz waves down the road to Aston, still leading the way. "Almost nothing at all. When the next car comes along, and we duck into the bushes, you just keep on hiking until someone stops."

"Then what?"

"We'll take over everything from there. It all depends on who and what kind of vehicle stops."

Jon turns away from Chaz to face Elizabeth. "You sure? Are you okay with this?"

The morning sunlight begins to shine brightly through the trees and she nods while staring off down the roadway. "I'm the one who got us all into this, so I can at least do my part to try and get us out."

A bit further down the road, Aston calls out to them. "Heads up! If dat is da newest plan, it is comin' on here fast."

As the sound of a big truck, shifting through its gears, thunders toward them, Elizabeth grumbles, "Aww, great... Why does it have to be a trucker?"

Chaz chuckles and pats her kindly on the shoulder. "Don't commend yourself too much... He hasn't stopped yet." She gives him an insulted look, as the three men scurry off into the roadside underbrush.

~*~

From behind the steering wheel of a banana delivery truck, a Jamaican lorry driver jams to loud reggae music. Hands waving, he dances while driving the stake-bed vehicle. Bouncing on the springy bench seat, he looks down the two-lane blacktop, as unkempt bushes whizz by on both sides. Cresting a small hill, the driver peers through the dirty windshield and notices the blond hair of a female hitchhiker.

Not believing his eyes, he reaches forward to clean the inside of his window with a rag. Approaching too quickly, the truck swerves into the grassy ditch and nearly runs over the blonde hitchhiker in the process. The woman jumps away from the vehicle's swerving path, and the driver slams on the brakes. The truck tires lock up and skid to a screeching stop. Looking out his side-view mirror, the driver sees that the attractive woman is unharmed but obviously taken aback.

The stunned trucker pushes open his driver's side door, hops out and runs back to check on her. "I'm so sorry, missus! You okay der?" As he comes around to the rear of the banana truck, he sees Elizabeth take a seat at the side of the roadway. He smiles, licking his tongue over his teeth as he approaches. "Hello, lady. You need a ride?"

A stealthy figure slips in behind the truck driver and grips a firm hand on his shoulder. Chaz whispers, soft and low, into the surprised trucker's ear. "Sure thing, sweetie. We'll be glad to have you give us a ride..."

Wide-eyed, the trucker looks behind at the grease-painted face of the man still retaining a firm grip on his shoulder. "Who is you?"

"Just a guy friend..."

Aston and Jon tumble out from hiding in the bushes, and the amazed driver glances over to look at them. "She sure got a lot of friends. Me have no bananas or cash."

Pressing the barrel of the handgun into the man's back, Chaz coaxes the driver away from the road to the passenger side of the empty truck. As everyone gathers together, he asks, "How would you like to take us to Port Antonio?"

"I was der just dis mornin' to unload me bananas."

Chaz keeps his persuasive hold on the man's shoulder. "Maybe you forgot something?"

"Like what?"

Still holding the gun, Chaz releases his grasp on the man's shoulder and pulls a twenty dollar bill from his pocket. "A tip, maybe?"

The truck driver looks back at him cleverly. "Ya, mon. Maybe I did forget sometin'… Like, forty bucks?"

Chaz grins and nods. "Yeah, I think that's what it was."

The now-cooperative driver puts on a beaming smile. "If da pretty lady comes up front wit me, I do it for thirty…"

Elizabeth steps up, as Chaz considers the deal. She frowns and shakes her head at him. "Don't you pimp me out."

"We might need the extra ten bucks later…"

Jon shakes his head at his military pal, while Aston steps up batting his eyelids in a mockingly flirtatious fashion. "Dey used to tink I was da pretty one, when I lived on da island here, long time ago."

The trucker stares at the scraggly beard on Aston and shakes his head. "It must'a been a long, long, long time ago for you to look like dis now."

Chaz moves to the rear bumper of the vehicle and ushers Jon and Elizabeth into the stake-bed of the old truck. He tilts his head to Aston and gestures toward the front cab. "You ride shotgun."

"Da beauty seat is okay-fine wit me."

The trucker continues to stare at the odd person with the familiar island accent. "Who is dis guy?"

The Navy SEAL steps forward and replies, "He'll ride in front with you to keep you honest. I'll give you the forty bucks when you drop us at our hotel."

The truck driver responds, "How about thirty now?" Chaz hands him a twenty dollar bill and tucks his gun away. "Here's a Jackson, and you get the rest when we arrive safe."

The trucker eagerly takes the American money and buries it deep in the front pocket of his cut-off denim shorts. "All aboard da Banana Express! Watch for da spiders der."

Opening the passenger side door, the truck driver climbs in and slides down the bench to sit behind the wheel. Aston follows behind him and pulls the door closed, as the diesel engine fires up again. Through the small rear window, the trucker sees his passengers make their way over the wood-rail sides to the open bed of the banana truck.

The trucker knocks on the glass and waves at them. When Chaz offers a thumbs-up sign, the driver pushes his foot to the clutch and shifts into low gear. Looking curiously at Aston's beard and unruly hair, he asks, "You say dat you live here in Jamaica?"

"In my youth for a spell."

The truck driver checks his mirrors, pushes on the gas pedal and cranks the steering wheel a few times to make a wide U-turn in the roadway. "You stay in dat jungle too long, my friend." The truck accelerates, then shifts through the gears and rumbles down the main road toward Port Antonio.

XXVII

At a low altitude, the Grumman seaplane buzzes along the coastline, looking for the boat carrying Jon and his friends. Rollie peers out the window at the remote island scenery and murmurs loudly. "C'mon… Where the heck are you guys?" Skirting around Navy Island, the seaplane does a low-level flyover and continues to follow the uninhabited shoreline. "This is not the kind of island sightseeing I want to be doing, down here in drug-smuggling territory."

~*~

Trailed by a black cloud of diesel exhaust, the banana truck rumbles into town. The human cargo in back keeps out of sight, as they cruise toward the hotel. Inside the truck cab, the driver looks over at his passenger and then out the side window to the Japanese import car parked directly in front of the hotel entrance.

There is a tap on the cab's rear window, and the trucker looks back to see Chaz shaking his head, pointing forward, and silently mouthing, "Marina."

Confused, the truck driver peers at Aston and asks, "Who dis Maria?"

Aston looks back at Chaz, as the Navy SEAL points down the street toward the harbor. "I tink he say go to da marina instead."

The driver nods with a smile. "Yes, mon. Dat makes much more sense." Shifting the gears, the truck jolts and belches exhaust as they continue down the busy street toward the Errol Flynn Marina.

~*~

The port seems unusually quiet, as the delivery truck rumbles up to the parking area and rolls to a creaking stop. Chaz pokes his head up over the slats of the truck box, looks around for any of the Booty Gang and then ducks down again.

Elizabeth leans her back against the cab. Jon, squatting next to her, queries Chaz, "You see anyone out there?"

"No one is around… That's what troubles me."

Elizabeth watches Chaz scan the marina through the gap between the slats and asks, "You think it's a trap?"

"I always think it's a trap. That's why I'm still alive."

After exchanging a troubled expression with Elizabeth, Jon turns to Chaz and whispers. "What are you thinking we should do?" He looks around the mostly empty truck bed and sees something moving under some banana leaves in the corner. "I don't really want to hang around in the back of this truck waiting for our ride home."

Chaz peeks out the slatted truck sides and studies the various boats tied at the docks. "I can see our boat is back in its berth."

Jon scoots forward and leans down to look at the pier. "It's good to know Desmond made it back okay last night." Chaz turns to look at him, and then suggests, "I think we need to get back to the other side of that island, where your seaplane friend can find us."

Elizabeth is not too keen on the idea. She looks at Jon and then back to Chaz. "You mean to where the gangsters took us hostage?"

Jon nods his agreement. "It does seem pretty likely that they would find us before Rollie does."

Chaz frowns as he looks to the seemingly vacant pier. "The odds aren't good, are they?"

From the front of the truck, they hear the passenger-side door open and close. The three in back peek through the wood-slats and see Aston walking to the pier. He strolls down the waterfront toward the dock and casually glances around.

Elizabeth looks at the two men beside her and gasps, "What is he doing?"

Chaz shushes her and whispers, "Forward scout..." They watch, as Aston walks down the pier, climbs into the chartered fishing boat and disappears from sight.

A short time later, Aston appears again with a hand lifted high to show a single key dangling from a floating fob. He smiles and gestures them over to the waiting watercraft. Jon looks aside to Chaz and mutters, "Is the boat really our best chance?"

Chaz looks at their quiet surroundings and shrugs. "Seems better off than this empty truck bed..."

Already climbing over the side of the truck rails, Elizabeth drops down to the street and whispers back to them. "C'mon, guys. If we're going, let's get to it."

Jon grimaces, as he watches his military friend proceed to climb out and join her. "This is not how I would write this particular scenario."

From the opposite side of the truck, Chaz smiles at Jon as he climbs down. "If you ever wrote down this kind of stuff, no one would even believe you."

He tosses another twenty dollar bill through the window of the cab and waves to the appreciative driver. "Hey, buddy… Thanks for the lift."

"No problem, mon!"

Jon climbs out of the truck, joins Elizabeth on the pavement and looks toward the marina. "The boat it is…?"

She replies, "Unless you can see another way…"

They look at each other with uncertainty and, with a shrug of acceptance, watch Chaz jog to the boat dock.

XXVIII

With Aston standing behind the controls, the inboard twin-engines on the fishing boat start up. Elizabeth climbs inside, as Jon unties the bowline from the docking cleat. The Key Wester feathers the throttle. The motors rumble and he eases the craft forward to provide slack for the remaining line at the stern.

Chaz unfastens the last tie-line, jumps aboard and calls up to Aston. "Did you check if we have enough fuel?"

Smiling, Aston turns to the others and holds up a slip of paper with scribbled handwriting on it. "Our island friend, Desmond, left da keys wit'a note."

Jon takes the message from Aston and reads it aloud. *"Aston-mon, hope you enjoyed your visit. The tanks is topped off, compliments of my Mudda. D~"*

Everyone looks toward Aston, blushing through his deep tan as he throttles up the engines to pull away from the pier. "She was a lady-friend when I run 'round dese parts."

They watch from the stern as the banana truck billows a cloud of exhaust smoke pulling away from the marina.

Elizabeth coughs and takes a deep breath to fill her chest. "Wow, I thought we were going to die from the fumes coming up from under that truck."

Chaz sweeps his hand over the side of the boat, scoops some water in his cupped hand and wipes it across his face. "Never say die with a Navy SEAL around."

The watercraft motors away from the marina, and Jon looks ahead toward Navy Island. "That was an adventure."

Standing up, Chaz looks out past the helm and notices something in the crowd of vessels. "It seems the adventure is just beginning. Look over there!" He points to a familiar yacht, as it pulls away from the pier and strikes a course that follows in their wake.

Jon's jaw drops and he utters, "Damn… Why didn't we notice them tied up there before?"

Distraught, Elizabeth shakes her head and replies. "One boat is just like any other to me."

Chaz licks the salty water on his lips and wipes the moisture from his face. "You know what? That thought should've crossed my mind." He goes for the gun in his duffle and calls to the islander at the controls. "Aston, let's get going! We're gonna have some company!"

Peering over his shoulder, Aston spots the trailing yacht, turns to look ahead and pushes forward on the throttles. "And not da welcome kind!"

Picking up speed, the fishing boat races out of the marina, as the gangster yacht slowly makes its way from the crowd of boats at the pier. With his gun in hand, Chaz moves next to Aston and points to Navy Island, gesturing starboard. "Head around to the east of the island. We may be able to make some distance on them through the shoals, while they will have to keep to the deep water."

Throttles pushed full-forward, Aston turns the ship wheel and the boat veers to travel counterclockwise around the nearby island. Everyone in the boat looks behind to watch, as the larger yacht begins to pick up speed and swallow their trail with a much bigger wake. Nervously folding her arms, Elizabeth stares astern and asks, "Can we outrun them?"

Jon shakes his head. "I don't think so."

Intent, Chaz takes a quick breath. "They can go faster, but we can maneuver closer to the shore. It may be enough to keep us ahead of them, until we come up with another plan." The Navy SEAL looks to Jon and smirks.

Completely befuddled, Jon responds. "I suppose you think it's my turn to make the plan?"

"You're welcome to it."

~*~

Cruising around Navy Island, the smaller fishing boat stays closer to the jungled coastline, while the gangster yacht, further out, slowly closes the distance between them. On the northern coast of the island, out of view from the main harbor, the amphibious flying boat from Key West Air Charters sits parked on a stretch of white sand beach. The high-winged aircraft rests at the edge of the waterline, with gentle waves rolling in and lapping on its curved hull. Aston is the first to gleefully call out, "Der is da Rollie-mon!"

Jon sees the beached seaplane and raises his arm high. "Yes! Our ride is awaiting us!"

Gauging the distance between their boat and the yacht, Chaz estimates the timeframe for them to safely reach the seaplane. His calculation of their predicted position puts a grim expression on his face. He moves alongside Jon and Elizabeth and states, "No good... We won't make it."

The fishing boat bounces through the small waves. Elizabeth holds tightly to the side rail and replies to Chaz. "What do you mean? Can't he fly us?"

"The timing is all wrong. That bigger boat will have plenty of time to be on us before we could all get aboard the seaplane and get off the water."

Jon follows Chaz to the controls and watches, as he opens a side compartment to pull out an emergency flare kit. He looks at his friend questioningly. "What are you intending to do with that?"

"We need to get the attention of the pilot on that beach, but we can't stop for a chat." He takes the flare from the storage case and loads the single, oversized barrel of the gun. Chaz gives the emergency device a twirl on his index finger, hands it over to Jon, and then moves behind the controls. "Thanks Aston, I can take over the driving from here on out." Aston offers a casual salute and steps aside to look through the port windows toward the seaplane resting on the beach. Chaz takes the ship wheel and hollers out orders, as he steers the fishing boat through the much shallower coastal waters. "Jon, take that flare and shoot over the seaplane on the beach. That should get your pilot friend's attention!"

The boat bounces across the water at full speed, and Jon makes his way forward to the bow with the signal flare. He points the barrel to the sky above the island and looks back to Elizabeth and Chaz. "After he sees this… Then what?"

Holding tight, as they bounce across the water, everyone looks to Jon with the emergency flare and then over to the beach with the seaplane. Elizabeth nervously remarks, "Hopefully, he follows us."

Rocking the ship wheel to angle through the waves, Chaz nods and jabs a finger in Jon's direction. "Fire it!"

XXIX

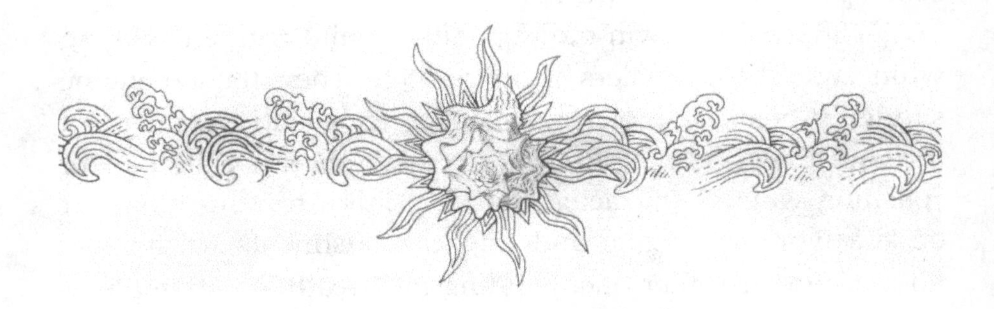

On the shore, lounging in the shade of a palm tree, Rollie gazes out at blue ocean waters and his seaplane lazing peacefully at the edge of the secluded beach. He hears the distant sound of a boat motor coming from the east end of the island and sits up as the sound nears. Slowly climbing to his feet, he swats the dry sand from the seat of his pants, squints to the horizon and thinks to himself, "I hope that's not the Jamaican Coast Guard." The fishing boat finally comes into view and Rollie quickly recognizes it from the day prior. "You're coming on kind of fast guys..." He watches, as the wooden boat zips across the shallows at full throttle and then notices the yacht coming around the bend in deeper waters and paralleling their path.

Suddenly, smoke from a signal flare shoots out from the bow of the lead boat. Leaving a trailing arc through the air, the flaming projectile hits the beach just behind the tail section of the seaplane, then skitters across the sand into the bushes. Wide-eyed, the pilot exclaims, "What the hell was that for?!?"

He dashes across the empty beach and hustles inside through the rear hatch of the seaplane. Looking back out at the boats, he speculates, "I guess we're not stopping to see the sights…" The rear cargo door swings closed and, with a clank, the inside latch fastens shut. The tilted wings of the seaplane shift as the pilot maneuvers inside.

Shortly, the twin radial engines ignite with a chugging whine, and the propellers begin to rotate. Then, the left engine suddenly belches smoke and chokes to a halt. Looking out through the windows, Rollie helplessly observes the pair of speeding watercrafts racing by. He adjusts the throttle lever on the working engine and makes adjustments to the fuel mixture for the other one. Holding his breath, he attempts to start the left engine again. He watches, as the propeller spins slowly and a cloud of black exhaust pours from the engine cowling. "Dammit, Ace! You were supposed to fix that!" Through the port window, he notices Aston waving from the stern of the fleeing boat. Adjusting the engine throttle again, Rollie swears out loud as the yacht advances on the smaller boat, "C'mon, dammit!"

The left engine attempts to start, with the propeller spinning until the engine finally catches and comes to life. Cracking a smile of relief, Rollie cheers it on. "That's it, baby!" With both engines rumbling and both propellers spinning, the amphibious seaplane slowly eases forward away from the beach and into deeper surf.

~*~

From the stern of the boat, Aston watches as they race around Navy Island trying to evade the pursuing gangsters. He looks over to Chaz at the boat controls and announces, "Dat Rollie-mon is off da beach now 'nd he's comin' after us." Standing next to each other, Jon and Elizabeth exchange a nervous glance. She crinkles her brow apprehensively, and looks back at the seaplane departing the island. Her gaze moves to the pursuing yacht that is quickly gaining on them. "How is this supposed to play out exactly?"

Jon leans forward to Chaz and asks, "Hey there buddy, what was that new plan of yours again?"

Preoccupied, the Navy SEAL jogs the steering wheel to swerve around a shallow sand bar and then looks back at Jon. "I thought we said it was your turn to make up the plan…"

~*~

Navigating the shallow waters around Navy Island, the fishing boat rounds the western shore to approach the main island of Jamaica again. Seeing the Port Antonio bay in the distance, Chaz skirts the smaller boat away from the mouth of the harbor and steers west along the mainland coastline toward Ocho Rios.

The gangster yacht follows to the west, cutting their angle of approach toward the fleeing boat, and the waterborne seaplane follows in their wake. Splashes of water hiss off the hot engines and spray through the spinning props, as the seaplane slowly gains on the yacht. Two men appear on deck to observe as the seaplane approaches.

A wave splashes against the forward windshield of the seaplane, as Rollie tries to find smoother water for a take-off. He offers a friendly wave to the crewmen at the stern of the yacht, and they withdraw as the plane steadily races closer. The two gang members promptly return, each with an automatic machine gun.

Rollie's composed expression turns to alarm. He slams the overhead throttles forward, making the radial engines scream with strain. "Don't you bastards shoot my airplane!" The crewmen position the automatic-rifles to their shoulders, as the seaplane suddenly lifts from the water and zooms over their heads within a few feet of the yacht's bridge.

The men cower to the deck and look up as the seaplane roars past. In their momentary window of opportunity, they spray several rounds of machine gun bullets skyward. Thundering overhead, the seaplane takes up position between the two racing watercrafts.

~*~

The fishing boat smashes into consecutive sets of swells perpendicular to their course, and the boat loses forward momentum on each jarring impact. Chaz steers the boat as close to the coast as he safely can without scraping the bottom. He looks aside to Jon. "Where is that seaplane pilot buddy of yours when we need him?"

Just as Chaz finishes speaking, Jon points behind to where the flying boat leapfrogs between the vessels and drops down to only a few feet above the water. "There he is!"

The seaplane stays low over the surface of the water as it comes steadily up behind the speeding boat. Impressed, Chaz smiles at Jon and then turns ahead to steer. "Hot damn, that's some good flying!"

"Hey Chaz, you were saying something about his being where we need him… Now, how do we get aboard?"

A rogue swell of water slams into the side of the small boat and engulfs the vessel. Everyone holds tight as water splashes over them and jostles them from secure footing. Clinging to the ship's wheel, Chaz looks back, counts heads, and climbs back to his feet. "Don't anyone fall out now!"

Jon helps Elizabeth to her feet and she hugs him tightly. She looks to the seaplane and then to the yacht closing the distance behind them. "Jonathan… Our situation hasn't really improved much…!"

Jon grasps her around the waist and, over the combined noise of the aircraft and boat engine, hollers to the boat driver. "What now, Chaz?"

Chaz swipes the splash of seawater from his beard. "Wave your pal to our starboard side, and I'll match up our bow with his rear-hatch cargo door."

In complete shock, Jon replies "Seriously?!?"

Shaking her head in disbelief, Elizabeth exclaims, "What! Are you nuts? You must be joking!"

Chaz swerves the boat, and the hull smashes into the swelling water before launching across to another set of big waves. "Do you have any better ideas?"

XXX

Despite the loud roar of the seaplane engines behind them, Jon hears the distinct popping sounds of gunfire coming from the yacht in pursuit. Elizabeth stands frozen in shock, and Jon joins Aston at the rear of the fishing boat to wave Rollie in. Trying to convey his message, Jon motions with his arms toward the starboard side of the boat. The pilot responds with a thumbs-up through the windshield.

The aircraft tilts its wings to the right and veers off, just as a spray of hostile gunfire erupts from the pursuing yacht. Aston pulls Jon to the deck, and the bullets smack into the stern of the wooden boat with a series of hollow *plinks*.

Scampering low across the deck of the boat, Jon rushes to Elizabeth and pulls her down to safety. "You okay, Lizzy?"

With apprehension, she looks over to him and answers back, "I'm not hurt, but I'm definitely not okay." They both watch in awe, as the low-flying seaplane skims over the water's surface alongside the speeding boat and then pulls up ahead on the starboard bow.

Chaz hollers back to them at the stern. "Get your gear and get up there!"

The wind blows Aston's hair and beard back, as he climbs to the upper cabin deck. He reaches for Elizabeth's bag and ushers her onward to the forward bow of the fleeing boat. Jon grabs his backpack and moves to join them, but turns back to ask Chaz. "What about you?"

"Someone has to drive the boat."

Jon shakes his head. "I'm not leaving you here."

The Navy SEAL smiles and looks back at the pair of thugs ineffectively firing their automatic machine guns. "These amateurs are nothing compared to the bad-guys I've had to deal with in the Middle East. If I can get you away safe, I can easily slip out on my own."

They both turn to look ahead, as Aston helps Elizabeth move forward to the bow of the bouncing craft. They look to the airborne seaplane zooming alongside, and Jon shakes his head. "No, we should all stay together."

"Jon, your responsibility is to get her away from here. I'll be just fine."

"This plan really sucks!"

Chaz grins amiably. "Hell, it's not much of a plan, and who knows if it will even work out?"

"Come up there with us."

Holding the ship wheel tight and trying to maneuver up closer to the hovering seaplane, Chaz shakes his head. "Won't work. Now go up there and jump in that seaplane!"

Jon starts to move forward and yells back to Chaz. "You act like I've never done anything like this before!"

Chaz laughs, as Jon climbs to the upper deck and makes his way forward. Watchful of his steering of the boat, Chaz tries to match speed with the plane hovering at the bow.

His voice gets swept away in the breeze, as he wonders aloud, "Damn Jon… Have you…?"

Just off the starboard bow, the seaplane drops dangerously close. The passengers on the boat cling to the bow, as the seaplane's prop-wash blows back against them. Handing Elizabeth his backpack, Jon crouches low and steps forward toward the seaplane's rear cargo door.

Knees bent on the bouncing deck of the fishing boat, Jon creeps forward and warily reaches out to the airplane, just before him. Like a stunt wing-walker from barnstorming days, he slowly scoots up and grabs the handle on the cargo door.

The hatch unlocks and the door swings open, knocking Jon from his footing. He slides across the boat deck and holds tight to the door handle, then slips from the surface of the forward bow before dangling over the water below. The low-flying seaplane maintains a steady altitude at the slow airspeed, then dips down to bounce off the water's surface. Jon's feet touch the water, and one of his shoes tumbles away into the seaplane's wake.

From the front of the fishing boat, Elizabeth screams, "Hold on, Jon!!!" She looks back through the cabin window to Chaz, who carefully tries to maneuver the bow of the boat closer to the tail section of the water-skimming aircraft.

From the cockpit, Rollie looks back to the cargo hold and notices the wind is blowing things around near the open hatch. He can just barely make out the figure of Jon clinging outside the rear doorway. "Shit! Hang in there, buddy…!" Skimming only a few feet over the tips of the waves, Jon's dangling feet splash several more times before the bouncing bow of the fishing boat returns to its position under the seaplane's tail section.

Dropping back onto the front deck of the speeding boat, Jon looks up at the airplane just a few feet away.

Elizabeth hurriedly crawls up beside him and hugs him close. "Jon, are you okay?"

"I can hardly believe it, but I've done enough of that in the past few weeks to last a lifetime." He shakes his wet, shoeless foot and takes one of the backpacks from Aston. Positioned at the front of the boat, they continue to bounce along below the tail section of the seaplane and Jon smiles at Elizabeth. "I'll be okay when you're safely aboard that plane." He slings one of their bags through the open rear hatch door and grabs for the other.

Aston moves in behind them, and they huddle in the prop-wash from the seaplane. Looking back at the yacht crew still shooting at them and getting ever-nearer, Aston shouts, "It be dat time to go?!?" Jon nods and gestures to the airplane hovering over them. "You get aboard first and help her."

Aston moves forward, reaches up to the airplane and pulls himself aboard. He makes the boat-to-aircraft transfer look surprisingly easy and Jon exchanges a look of astonishment with Elizabeth. Taking her by the arm, Jon supports her, as she reaches with her other hand to the hatch. "You see! Just like that… No problem!"

Eyes wide, Elizabeth looks at Jon and tilts her head. "You made it look a bit more difficult!"

Jon tosses the other bag through the hatch door to Aston and then urges her forward. "C'mon, I'll help you."

Several more rounds of machine-gun fire snap off from the pursuing yacht, and the fishing boat swerves to the side, knocking them both from their feet. Bracing himself on a knee, Jon holds Elizabeth steady at the forward bow of the boat. Chaz hollers ahead to them. "You don't have to marry her! Just get her aboard!"

Jon looks back to Chaz and yells, "This isn't as easy as it looks!" The military man at the ship wheel merely shrugs and waves him onward.

Stabilizing her on the starboard bow of the boat deck, Jon inches slowly forward right behind Elizabeth. They move further up, behind the airplane's engine, and splashes from the propeller-wash blows hard against them. Supporting her around the waist as she reaches for the seaplane, Jon yells over her shoulder. "Easy does it…!"

Elizabeth reaches out to the hatch opening and the sinewy arm of Aston extends to take a firm hold of her hand. She puts up her other hand to grab at the doorway, just as the fishing boat hits another swell that bounces the vessel aside. Using the jolting momentum of the watercraft, Jon heaves Elizabeth upward and shoves her aboard the seaplane.

Launched inside, Elizabeth clears the hatch doorway. The seaplane dips down to skim the rolling waves, as the boat veers over and nearly collides with the aircraft's tail section. Taking advantage of the opportunity, Jon dives into the plane.

The flying boat lifts from the surface of the ocean again, and Jon braces himself at the threshold of the hatch doorway. He calls out to his friend on the boat, "Chaz, you can make it!" To Jon's dismay, the Navy SEAL waves a military salute and cranks the ship wheel to port. The boat peels away from the seaplane and veers off toward the Jamaican shoreline.

From the cockpit, Rollie leans over and hollers back. "Hey Springer… What about your pal?" As he makes a quick assessment of his passengers, a steady burst of machine-gun fire strikes the fishing boat and then is redirected toward the low-flying airplane.

Jon reaches outside and swings the cargo hatch closed, as several bullet *ting* against the metal skin of the seaplane. Jon yells ahead to the pilot, "Go, go, go! We're all aboard."

Rollie peers back from the cockpit to see the door close. He pulls back on the yoke, as he throttles up both engines and then banks the seaplane up and away from the volley of gunfire. Over the roar of the airplane engines, Rollie calls out to those in the cargo hold. "The passenger list seems light… But, I'm okay with it if you are."

Jon secures the latch on the door and moves to one of the port-side windows to stare out at the Jamaican shoreline. He watches the fishing boat run aground on a slender patch of white, sandy beach. From the boat, a backpack-wearing figure leaps ashore, dashes away and disappears into the jungle.

A look of dread suddenly washes over Jon's features, and he looks at Elizabeth. "Uh, Lizzy, did you ever get that treasure back from Chaz?"

Dismayed, she looks at her bag and shakes her head. "Actually, I'm still in a bit of shock at still being alive."

Jon moves across the cargo hold to sit beside her, and Aston makes his way up front to sit in the copilot chair. Elizabeth puts her hand on Jon's arm to offer some comfort. He lowers his chin to his chest and shakes it unhappily. "Lizzy, I'm sorry… This was all for nothing."

She gives his arm a squeeze and smiles while her eyes twinkle with delight. "Jon, there is a good reason that ninety percent of this job is research in the library."

He grins at her in return. "That's the way I thought it was supposed to be for my writing work, too…"

"Isn't it?"

"Not lately."

The seaplane lifts higher into the scattered clouds, and the coastline of Jamaica fades on the horizon behind them.

XXXI

The Key West Air Charters seaplane soars over blue ocean waters, as the coastline of Cuba comes into view to the north. Jon steps up, pokes his head into the cockpit, looks to Aston and then to the pilot. Jon turns his gaze to stare ahead at the approaching shoreline on the horizon. "What are we going to do about that?"

Rollie looks at Jon, and then peers down at the panel of instruments, letting his attention linger on the fuel gauge. "We're gonna have to put down and refuel."

Jon looks at the pilot like he must be joking. "What?"

"I wasn't able to properly refuel back in Jamaica."

Leaning in from the threshold of the cargo hold, Jon looks to Aston in the copilot seat and then back to the pilot. "Rollie, I thought you said he doesn't even have a passport…"

After assessing the fuel level, Rollie adjusts their altitude to lower on the approach. "Not my main problem right now."

Jon looks back to Aston. "We'll get thrown in jail."

"No time in da Cuba jail-place for me. Been der once 'fore and don't recommend it. B'sides, I've a boxing exhibition in Key West at da Conch tonight."

The nervous passenger turns back to the pilot again. "Am I missing something here?"

The seaplane drops low over the water and zooms toward the beach on a flight path similar to the prior Cuban fly-over. Rollie adjusts his butt in the seat, readying for more tree-top flying and tilts his head toward Jon. "Just sit tight, grab a drink, and take it easy with that good-lookin' blonde back there. I'll let you know when we are about to put down."

Shaking his head, Jon glances back at Elizabeth, who is holding onto her seat as the seaplane dives toward the beach. "Rollie, is this another one of your *long* approaches?"

The plane buzzes over the narrow strand of beach, scattering flocks of birds as it flies just above the foliage.

~*~

The ocean beyond the northern coast of Cuba comes into view ahead of them, and Rollie pulls back the overhead throttles. The engines chug, as if starved for fuel and Rollie glances over to Aston. "Not sure if this is a good idea…"

The islander shrugs and looks out the starboard window at rocky cliffs surrounding a beach-rimmed cove just coming into view. "When you don't have a choice, it doesn't matter much if da idea is good or not."

Glancing down at the fuel indicator, Rollie watches the needle bounce at the lowest level. He looks out the window as they pass over the sheltered cove, and then he banks the airplane and comes around again. "Alright gang, there it is." The pilot leans over and yells back to Jon and Elizabeth. "Strap in! We're going to put down on the water soon."

Jon pulls his seatbelt tighter and calls up to the cockpit. "How is the fuel supply?"

Rollie smirks. "What fuel? That's the whole reason we're going down." The pilot gives a half-hearted thumbs-up, while Jon and Elizabeth look to each other with concern.

~*~

The amphibious seaplane flies past the landmass of Cuba and drops low over the ocean water. As it passes by the rocky, cliff-side beach, it enters a tranquil, protected harbor. The seaplane banks its wings, comes around, and drops onto glassy waters alongside a large pleasure yacht with the name ***Anastasia*** lettered across the recently repainted stern.

Water splashes up on the windshield, as the flying boat touches down and step-taxis toward the waiting ocean vessel. At the upper railing of the yacht, Carlos, with a cigar clasped between his thumb and forefinger, appears in his usual Caribbean island-chic outfit. He takes a long drag and waves a greeting to the approaching aircraft.

Rollie looks beside at his copilot, Aston, and grumbles. "This is going to cost me a lot more than a few jugs of fuel."

"Dats da way of da world."

"Yeah, it's never what it appears."

"Yes, Rollie-mon… Especially with Carlos."

~*~

The seaplane cruises over to the anchored yacht, and the spinning propellers power down to a low idle. The nose hatch of the plane swings open, and Aston's head pops up. Carlos smiles at the sight of the familiar island character. "Ahh, a reunion of old friends."

Aston waves a hand and tosses a tether rope over to the boatman at the stern. Jorge begrudgingly catches the line and looks to Carlos, waiting until he receives an approving nod. Given the go-ahead, the Cuban henchman pulls the seaplane closer and fastens the rope to connect the two floating vessels.

~*~

From inside the seaplane, Rollie can see Jorge fastening their tether line to a cleat. He peers back over his shoulder at his two passengers and sighs. "Believe it or not, it's Carlos to the rescue on this one…"

Unbuckling and rising from his seat, Jon steps forward and bends to look out the round-topped windshield. He sees the Cuban businessman with a cigar on the deck of the yacht. Confused, he looks to Rollie, while the pilot shuts down both engines. "I thought you told me to never trust him?"

"That is good advice that I'm unfortunately not able to follow today." Rollie folds up an aerial map and tucks it away. He shifts to the copilot seat and scrunches down to squeeze through the narrow crawlspace leading up to the nose hatch. "If Carlos brought all the fuel that I asked for, it will take me a bit of time to transfer it over to this bird."

Jon looks to the unfriendly, hulking form of Jorge at the stern railing. "How long will we be in Cuban waters?"

Bending down to make his way forward, Rollie grunts, "Not any longer than we have to."

Coming up from behind, peeking over Jon's shoulder, Elizabeth watches the seaplane pilot disappear into the nose compartment. She looks outside, just as Aston climbs over to the rear deck of the yacht. She whispers softly in Jon's ear. "Traveling with you is a lot like holding your breath between exciting chapters of your books."

He glances back at her. "Believe me, I much prefer writing this stuff than living it." She grins understandably and rests her hand on his arm. They both feel a tingle of exhilaration as they reflect on what they've been through.

Jon heaves a weary breath before bending down to crawl forward toward the nose hatch. "Just follow after me. Wait until you meet this fellow, Carlos."

Elizabeth looks outside to the big yacht and the well-dressed Cuban with the cigar protruding from his pursed lips. She smiles and watches Jon scrunch down under the instrument panel. "He seems like a nice enough fella…"

XXXII

The sun is high in the sky, as Jon and Elizabeth sit with Carlos on the deck of the Cuban yacht. Jorge, the henchman, accompanies the already-served cocktails with a silver tray of finger sandwiches. Their Cuban host is enamored with his female guest and edges closer to her.

From over the deck railing, Jon watches Rollie and Aston fill the plane with fuel from the dozen metal canisters lined up like dominoes along the stern of the luxury boat. Elizabeth backs away from Carlos and looks to Jon, hoping to be rescued from the close encounter. She clears her throat. "Jon… Mister Murietta says that, for some reason, you chose not to accompany him on his last trip to his home in Cuba?" Jon glances over and frowns at Carlos.

She looks at her writer friend strangely. "I thought you always wanted to go to Cuba. Sounds like a fun adventure…"

As Jon steps over to them, he notices Carlos' cat-like Cheshire grin of innocence. "It wasn't a well-planned outing, so I only made it halfway."

Amused, the crafty Cuban giggles at Jon. He smiles warmly at his confused female guest. Puffing on his cigar, Carlos retorts, "You know how these writer-types always want to go back and edit their mistakes."

Jon looks to the surrounding cliffs and the narrow beach on the mainland. "Should we be worried about anyone finding out about us here?"

Carlos takes a sip from his iced cocktail and shrugs. "These days, Señor, you should always be concerned when you are in a foreign land without the proper authorization." The Cuban businessman finishes his drink, and Jorge promptly steps up to hand him a freshly-mixed cocktail. Carlos swirls the drink in hand and remarks. "Elizabeth tells me she is a researcher of historical artifacts."

Jon smiles to Elizabeth. "Miss Blackwright is a very smart lady and a top professional in her field of expertise."

She takes a nibble from one of the small sandwiches, and Carlos eyes her up and down, hungrily. "Yes, I see that, and she appears to possess other attractive attributes as well."

Unamused and too weary to be insulted, Elizabeth turns to their Cuban host. "I suppose you mean that as a sort of compliment?"

He smiles his signature grin and bows at the waist. "But of course, I do."

Drink in hand, Jon returns to the side rail and continues to watch the refueling. He calls down, as Aston hands over another canister to Rollie. "How long until you're finished?"

Carrying the fuel can, Rollie balances himself on the seaplane's nose and then walks up the mid-section of the divided front windows to the top of the wings. He looks to Jon on the boat and waves. "You got time to finish your drinks. Still got several to go… We'll be a few minutes yet."

Jon looks back at Carlos, while the smarmy Cuban continues to appreciate the lone female guest. He turns back to Rollie and winces. "We're ready to go whenever you are." Moving across the deck, Jon rejoins Carlos and Elizabeth, as the host takes her empty drink glass while retaining his hold on her hand.

"So… The lovely Miss Blackwright. Tell me all about your experiences with finding treasure…"

With her hand held firm in the Cuban's upturned palm, she smiles uncomfortably and glances at Jon upon his return. "I deal with historical artifacts more than treasure, per se."

Carlos nods, while he sets his drink aside and clenches the stout cigar in his teeth. "I see…" His eyes dart to Jon. "Weren't you in Jamaica looking for prized Spanish loot?"

Elizabeth is unsure as to how she should deal with their inquisitive host. She replies, "Uh, well… Most of my work is with the paperwork of acquisitions, but occasionally it takes me into the field."

With a cunning sparkle in his eye, the Cuban nods and inquires further. "Following a treasure map and having the Jamaican Booty Posse after you makes it seem as if you were on the hunt for something very valuable."

She puts on her most naive expression and responds. "We didn't really find anything."

Carlos narrows an eye at her intuitively, and smirks. "May I see the treasure map?"

Elizabeth looks over to Jon, who shrugs and retorts, "What map are you referring to, Carlos?"

A young familiar voice pipes up from behind them all. "Hey writer-man… Maybe something like this?"

Carlos glances over, grinning, and the rest of them turn to see Casey Kettles slide the treasure map from its envelope. Jon walks over to the conniving teenager and puts out his open hand, demanding the item's return. "Give me that back, you sneaky little thief."

Casey hands over the handwritten letter and envelope, but holds onto the map and unfolds it. Jon reaches out for it, but Jorge heaves a low grunt and steps forward menacingly. Casey giggles, as he examines the map's details. "Easy there, mister mainlander. Your foreign friend here didn't shanghai me on this boat ride to come up empty-handed."

Carlos smiles and extends his own hand. "Oh Casey, you little brothel-sprout. May I please see your discovery?"

The youth steps around Jon, smiles at Elizabeth, and hands over the map to Carlos. He jeers at Jon knowingly. "From the looks of your bags, not much of a success for you this trip either, I guess..."

Jon scrutinizes the young bag-snooper and replies, "How did you get aboard to go through our stuff?"

Carlos examines the map, looking closely at the X-spot, and then looks up to Jon and Elizabeth. "Not on the hunt for treasure you say?" Then, he looks aside to Casey and inquires, "Did you check all of their baggage and search the whole interior of the plane?"

The smirking youth shakes his head, as he adjusts his yellow-sunglasses. "Nothing much else hidden in there. Just some old-man underwear that might belong to Rollie or Ace." Casey lifts a playful eye to Elizabeth and smiles naughtily. "She has more attractive undergarments, though..."

Shocked by the behavior of the impish teenager, Elizabeth scolds. "Who are you to rifle through our stuff?"

Casey smiles and tosses Jon his expensive wristwatch. "Well hello, Elizabeth... *Lizzy* Blackwright. I'm Casey Kettles and that's what I do."

Flummoxed, Jon looks at the timepiece that he thought he had safely tucked away and then straps it onto his wrist.

He looks over at Elizabeth and offers a shrug of surrender. "Yeah, that's what he seems to do."

Casting his gaze past the railing to Aston and Rollie, who are finishing up with the refueling, Jon queries Casey, "How did you get past the both of them?"

The wily teenager lowers his sunshades onto his nose and rolls his eyes in boredom. "I've been slipping past those two gooney birds for years."

Looking down over the stern rail, Jon watches Aston place the last empty fuel canister aside while Rollie closes the wing tank on the seaplane. He calls to them. "Hey guys… How we doing down there?"

Rollie looks up to Jon and waves. "All set! Get aboard, and we'll get out of here."

When the teenage figure of Casey Kettles suddenly appears at the stern railing next to Jon, Rollie nearly slips and falls off the wing of the seaplane from the surprise. "Casey… What the hell are you doing here?"

Pushing up his sunglasses, Casey waves to the pilot. "Dang Rollie, I thought you would be overjoyed to see me since we just saved your bacon and kept you from having to paddle home."

The pilot's expression flushes with anger and embarrassment. He looks at Jon and then down to Aston who leans out from the yacht's stern, looking up toward Casey. Irritated, Rollie proclaims, "The kid can stay with the Cuban as far as I am concerned!"

Jon looks over to young Casey, who merely shrugs and snarkily replies, "It's customary to leave with whoever brought you, ain't it?"

"You're on your own kid."

"Always have been."

Aston shakes his head at the sight of the mischievous teenager looking down at them, as Rollie impatiently growls, "Jon…! Grab your special lady-friend, and let's get the heck out of here."

The pilot slides down the windshield to the seaplane's nose hatch and Casey waves a casual salute, just above his yellow sunshades. "Always nice to see you too, Daddy-o."

XXXIII

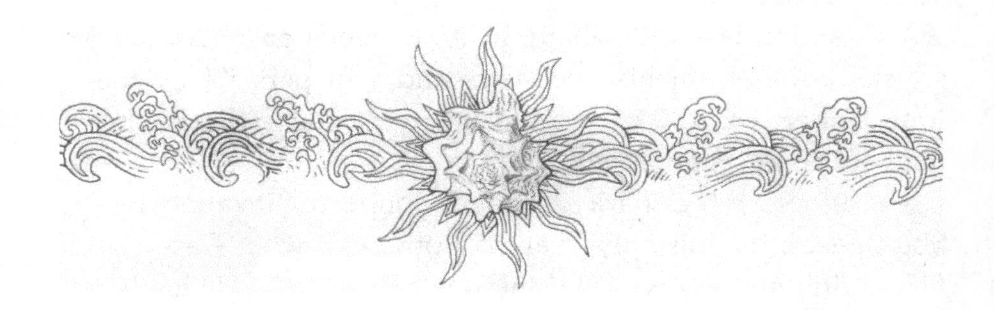

Jon turns away from Casey at the deck railing and walks back over to Carlos and Elizabeth. "C'mon, Lizzy. Our ride home is refueled and ready to go."

Holding the map, their cunning host looks at Jon. "Señor Springer, it is a happy occurrence that we encounter each other again so soon."

Hoping for the return of the treasure map, Jon holds his hand out. "Can we have that back, please?"

Snubbing out his cigar, Carlos bows his head and grins. "I would like to borrow it for a while. May I return it to you in Key West at a later date?"

Jon glances over at Elizabeth seeking her approval. Confounded, she replies. "Do we really have a choice?"

The Cuban puts on his familiar smile and tilts his head. "No, I'm afraid I will have to insist on it, Miss Blackwright. Consider it a partial payment for the smuggled fuel supplies." Jon tucks the letter in his pocket and reaches for her hand. "Elizabeth, the sooner we're away from this place, the better."

He looks back to Carlos and puts on a cordial smile. "Cuba that is... Not your lovely hospitality, of course."

"But of course." Carlos waves his hand with a flamboyant gesture and calls after them. "Consider it a loan, Señor Springer. I shall return it to you upon my next visit to your port of call."

As Jon leads Elizabeth away, he steps past Casey, who smirks, raises both his eyebrows and whispers, "Hey there, Mainlander... Can I have a crack at your lady-friend when I get back to the island?"

Ignoring the snarky teenager, Jon leads Elizabeth away. She pauses, having only heard a portion of what Casey said. "He didn't just say what I think he did, did he?" He leads her down the stairs to the rear deck and watches, as Rollie ducks down into the nose of the aircraft. "Yes... Yes, he did."

At the stern of the yacht, Jon and Elizabeth are greeted by Aston holding the tether line. They look through the windshield and watch as Rollie situates himself behind the controls and begins to go through his preflight checklist. Aston motions them aboard. "We's all fueled to go home."

Jon helps Elizabeth up to the front of the seaplane, and she slips down into the forward hatch. He looks back at Aston's smiling face and nods. "I guess it is home, now..."

"Home is jest where you are happy to return."

They see Elizabeth pop up between the chairs inside the cockpit and Rollie waves them both aboard. Jon climbs over the yacht's deck rail, to the nose hatch, and drops in, followed by Aston with the tether line.

Standing midway inside the forward hatch, like a centaur with a seaplane body, Aston pushes them away from the yacht. The flying boat drifts away, as Aston ducks down and pulls the hatch door closed. The coughing start of the radial engines is followed by a whining sound from the propellers as they begin to rotate.

The two engines finally catch and fire-up. Casey waves goodbye and smiles at Rollie, who stares out the side window. The pilot jabs a pointed index finger in the direction of the wayward youth. Casey returns the pointing gesture and then turns up his middle finger, waving it obnoxiously at the occupants of the seaplane. Disgusted, Rollie reaches up to adjust the throttles and turns the amphibious aircraft with a thrust of the starboard engine.

After watching the high-winged seaplane race from the cove and lift skyward, Carlos turns to Jorge and hands him the treasure map. "It seems that our work here is all done. Hide away those empty fuel canisters and set our course for the northern coast of Jamaica."

Casey climbs up the rear stairway to the upper deck and turns to Carlos. "Cool, I've never been to Jamaica."

The Cuban businessman smiles at the youngster. "Casey, my boy... I hope you know how dive with Scuba." Carlos takes up a fresh cocktail glass, stares out at the horizon and watches as the seaplane disappears from view.

~*~

On the tourist-crowded streets of Key West, Rollie's pickup truck weaves through the pedestrian and bike traffic. They follow behind Aston and his decorated beach cruiser, while the bird perched on his arm flaps its wings with delight. As they come around a corner, a Key West Police Jeep flashes on its emergency lights and pulls in behind them.

In the truck, Rollie looks past Elizabeth, seated between them, to Jon and snidely comments, "These island cops are always around when you don't need them."

Ahead, Aston looks back briefly, while his bird flaps its wings, and he continues to pedal down the crowded street.

Rollie steers the truck to the curb and peers out his side-view mirror. The police vehicle pulls up behind them and stops. The driver's door swings open, and an officer steps out.

Rollie squints into the bright, strobing lights, as the police officer walks forward and then stops at the tailgate of the truck. From the passenger side of the police vehicle, another person steps out and casually walks up alongside the pickup truck. Rollie turns to look out the dirty rear window and grunts, "Looks like we have a visit from a certain detective-friend."

Detective Lyle steps up to the passenger-side of the idling pickup truck and rests his hand on the open window. He bends down a bit to take a look inside. He sees Jon silhouetted by the bright flashing lights of the police vehicle and then his gaze travels over to Elizabeth, seated in the middle. The detective then looks to Rollie behind the wheel. "Hello there, Rollie."

The pilot stares ahead and replies. "Hello, Lyle."

"You just arrive back today?"

"Yep."

"Have you seen Carlos?"

Rollie looks over at Detective Lyle and puts on his best display of innocence in order to conceal any expression of guilt. "Carlos…? I've seen him a lot at the Conch Tavern."

The detective shakes his head and suspiciously eyes Elizabeth and then Jon. "How about you? Seen him of late?"

Jon replies. "Nope."

"How about your little pal, Casey?"

With a shrug, Jon answers again. "Nope."

Not surprised with the vague responses, Detective Lyle continues to scrutinize Jon while gesturing to the passenger in the middle. "She another out-of-town friend of yours?"

Jon nods briefly. "Yes. She is, sir." The detective shifts his scrutinizing gaze to Elizabeth and puts on a friendly smile. "Ma'am, you seem like a nice sorta lady. I wouldn't keep company with these two, if you want to keep out of trouble."

The lights from the police vehicle flash across her profile, as she turns and offers a warm smile to the detective. "Thanks for the warning, Officer."

Satisfied, Detective Lyle nods. "It's Detective, Ma'am." He looks back at Rollie. "You do any Cuban fly-overs lately?"

"Has there been any sightings?"

Tapping his palm on the truck's open window frame, Detective Lyle nods his head. "Yes, just a few..." The detective looks down the street and continues. "You brought Aston back just in time for his big showcase…"

Rollie shrugs his shoulders and reaches up to rest one of his hands on the steering wheel. "Headed there now."

"Okay, get on your way. We'll talk later about Carlos." Rollie gives a goodbye gesture, and the detective steps back from the window. The truck shifts into gear, rumbles forward onto the roadway and drives off. Standing in the rhythmic, flashing lights of the police vehicle, Lyle looks at the officer beside him and shakes his head. "Sometimes I think I've had enough of the Bubba-system around here." The officer doesn't respond, as he follows the detective back to their vehicle.

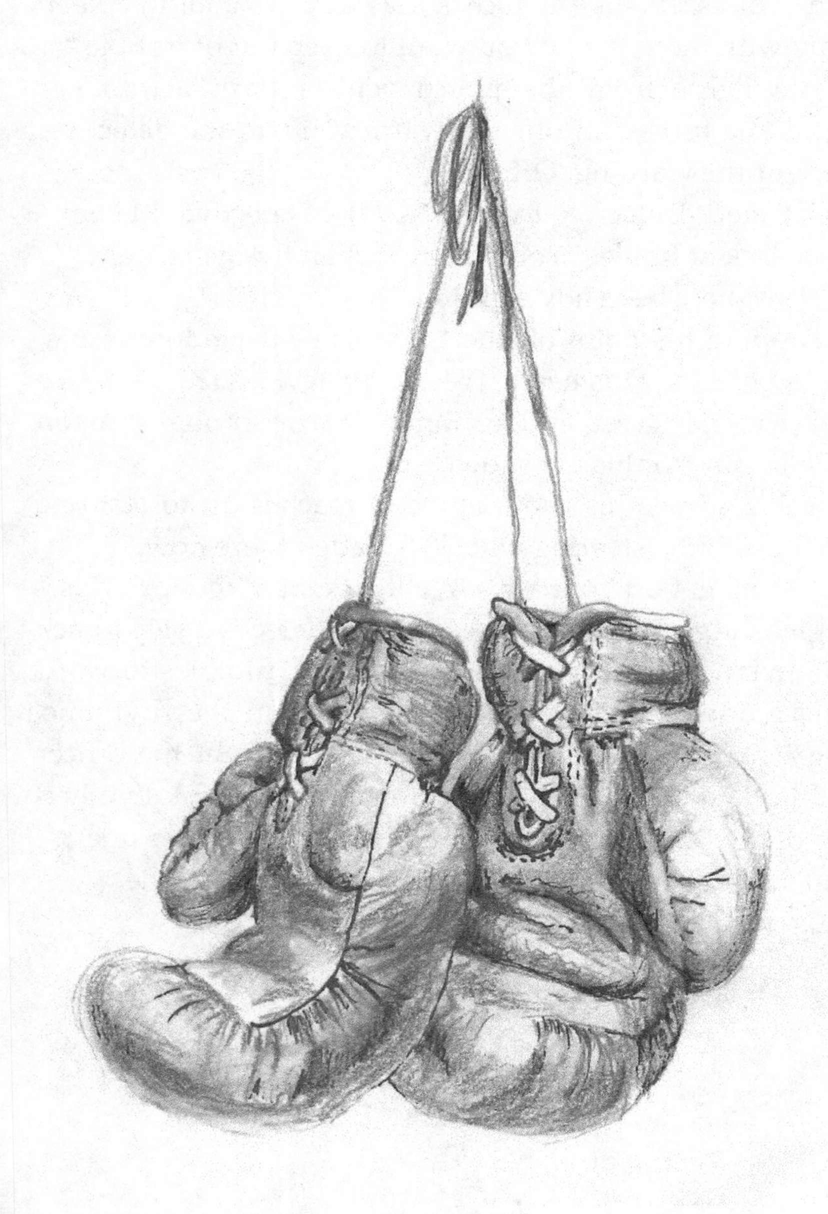

XXXIV

There is a makeshift boxing ring set up in the middle of the Conch Republic Tavern. Tables and chairs have been shoved to the perimeter, piled up high and pushed against the walls. In the standing-room-only spectator zone, surrounding the ring, are the majority of the barroom's Papa Hemingway incarnations with drinks in hand. Bounding to the center of the padded arena, Aston, bare-chested and bearded, holds a vintage pair of boxing gloves overhead. His parrot sits perched on a turnbuckle at the corner of the ring and squawks loudly while everyone cheers. When the noise finally abates, Aston announces, "Hallo der, you fans of Papa!"

The roar of the crowd increases, as they all raise their drinks to the portrait of Ernest Hemingway that is reverently displayed over the bar. Aston struts gamely around the perimeter of the fighting ring and holds out the padded leather gloves. He declares loudly, "I's da grandson of da man who spar'd wit da man hisself!" Holding the aged boxing mitts higher, Aston shows them around. The Papas cheer and make grunting noises, as he continues. "And dese are da same gloves dat bump da Papa 'nd soaked up many a pound of sweat from da old man."

Jon stands at the bar with Elizabeth and Rollie, while Angie moves back and forth serving drinks from behind the slab. From ringside, they hear Rollie's name being called out, and he turns to the pair beside him. "I've got to go help Aston give that boxing demonstration."

Polishing off his beer, the aviator sets it on the counter and makes his way through the cheering crowd. Ace comes over to fill his spot and greets Jon with a wink. "I thought y'all might be late." The mechanic chuckles and nods to Elizabeth. "It's rare that Rollie won't show to get his block knocked-off."

Angie leans on the bar with a smile. "Lookie here... The gang's all gathered to watch Aston give boxing pointers, while every Papa-wannabe in town takes a jab at Rollie."

Ace takes a swallow from his mug of beer and grunts. "I might buy a ticket myself. I only get a good chance once a year during these festivities."

Jon grins at the jesting mechanic and takes a sip from his own pint of beer. "It's good to be back here again."

Curious, Ace turns on a heel, puts and elbow to the bar, and lifts an eyebrow at Jon. "How did that engine work out?"

Jon exchanges a confidential glance with Elizabeth, and they both smile. "Everything worked out just fine." Satisfied, the mechanic bobs his head and makes his way through the crowd toward Rollie's corner of the boxing ring.

Elizabeth turns to Angie and orders another draft beer. She puts out some money, but the bar owner pushes it away. Angie picks up the empty glass, leans across the slab and puts her hand on Jon's shoulder. "Don't worry about it. I'll put your drinks on his tab. He needs more exciting folks in his life, so he can come up with some stories to write."

Embarrassed, Jon frowns at Elizabeth as she retorts. "He sure doesn't need *my* help being a prolific writer."

The bartender smiles sweetly and slides back behind the bar. "You just let me know when he writes something worth reading. I want a signed copy." Angie winks at her, causing her to glance over to Jon, puzzled. He bashfully shrugs it off without explanation, and Angie hands Elizabeth another pint of beer.

Jon sips his beer and looks back at the owner of the bar. "Elizabeth has always been supportive of my writing career."

The pair of old friends exchange an expression of sincerity, while Angie looks on with a trifling air of affectionate jealousy. The bartender leans over the bar again and places her hand on his shoulder. "You might want to keep her around. Just one look from her really lights you up."

Jon beams as he watches Elizabeth observe the Papa Hemingway boxing exhibition, and then he turns back to Angie. "We're just good friends."

"Those are the best kind to have around." Angie smiles at Jon perceptively and turns to fill another beer from the tap.

Despite the raucous cheering and loudness of the room, Jon watches Elizabeth enjoying the spectacle and feels a burning desire to be alone with her. She senses him observing her and turns to him with a smile. "You okay, Jon?"

He nods and hides behind taking a sip from his beer. "Yeah… It's been a long couple of days."

"Want to get out of here?" When Jon gives a tired shrug, Elizabeth places her drink on the bar and takes his hand. "Good, I need some fresh air."

The two weave their way through the crowd of tropical shirts and khaki. They pass Ace, ringside, who salutes them and hollers, "Springer, ever since you arrived, it's been out of the ordinary. I can't say I hope to see you again soon!"

From behind the bar, Angie watches as the two leave. Scooting their unfinished drinks from the slab, she makes room at the bar for other patrons. The cheering of the crowd and the solid smack of boxing mitts on flesh continues, as the Hemingway Days festivities carry on.

~*~

Stepping out into the much quieter night, Jon and Elizabeth move down the street toward Rollie's vehicle parked just around the corner. Jon opens the truck door and grabs their bags from the seat. He turns to Elizabeth, where she stands in the light of a streetlamp. A strange expression comes over her and she utters, "I just realized that I don't have a place to stay tonight."

Jon slings his pack over his shoulder and carries hers. "Where did you stay the other night when you were here?"

"At some old, historic residence named after a clipper-ship. Kitty something?"

He holds Elizabeth's bag and flushes, embarrassed. "The Clipped Kitty?"

"That's the place!"

"Who took you there?"

"Rollie said everywhere else was busy for the festival."

Slightly amused, Jon hooks her bag over his arm and ushers her down the street. "You can stay at my place."

She smiles provocatively. "Would that be proper?"

"You were going to put me up in Jamaica, right?"

"Yes, I guess I was."

Jon teases as they walk, "And your place was a mess."

Elizabeth moves closer to Jon, bumps her hip against him, and puts her arm through his. She quietly murmurs, "Yeah… I hope yours is much more presentable."

XXXV

The side streets and residential neighborhoods of Key West are mostly quiet during the later hours of the evening. Walking together, Jon and Elizabeth chat while enjoying the cool, night breeze. She looks at one of the uniquely built homes on the street and points to the triangle-shaped vent at the attic peak of the Conch-style house. "Why do most of the houses here have such character?"

"Everything on the island here has a lot of character."

As they walk, Elizabeth turns her gaze to Jon. Her eyes seem to sparkle despite the evening shadows. She softly replies, "Yes… I've met some of your new friends."

He smiles and responds, "They do make keeping to my writing-schedule a bit of a challenge…"

As they continue strolling down the street, Elizabeth leans her head over and rests it on his shoulder. "How long do you think you will stay down here?"

"I don't know… A while, I guess."

"You ever thinking of coming back to California?"

Jon shrugs and stares ahead as they continue walking. He adjusts the bag over his shoulder and keeps her held close to him. "How long can you stay here?"

"A few days... Maybe more, if I get some work done."

Looking up to the treetops under the starry night sky, Jon chuckles to himself and moves his body closer to hers. "That's what I told myself when I first arrived here."

She leans her cheek into him, while her eyes turn upward. "How far to your place?"

"It's just up here on the right."

~*~

Jon and Elizabeth enter through the yard gate and walk through the dark, shadowy gardens toward the garage apartment around back of the main house. She follows him up the spiral staircase, and he pulls open the creaking screen door. Noticing the entry was open and unlocked, she laughs. "Did you forget to lock up while you were out?"

Jon studies her in the moonlight for a moment before moving inside to a lamp. "I never found a key to the place." He switches on a table light near the door, which illuminates the apartment's interior.

Elizabeth looks around the tastefully decorated living area and steps further inside. Her fingertips brush over his computer on the table, and she makes her way to the island-themed, rattan couch. "So this is where the magic happens?"

"Nothing much of late..."

She stops before sitting and looks at him curiously. "Your new friends here don't seem to know anything about your writing..."

Jon shrugs nonchalantly, as he moves to the kitchenette. "I forgot to mention about *J. T. Springs*."

She glances over the leather-bound volumes of books on the shelf and turns to him. "You haven't told anyone?"

From the basket on the counter, Jon takes a small, green lime and squeezes it, testing for firmness. "Fresh start and all, I guess." He tosses the tiny lime in the air and catches it. "Would you like a drink?"

She grins. "Is that one of those Key Limes I've heard so much about?" She taps her fingers across the keys of the old, Royal Deluxe typewriter on the shelf and he nods.

Jon slices the lime and looks up at her. "Cuba Libre?"

"Yes, please."

Jon takes out two glasses, fills them with cubes of ice from the freezer and grabs a bottle of Conch Republic Rum. He fills each glass halfway with rum and takes a can of soda from the cabinet beneath the counter. Elizabeth smirks as she watches him. "What are you making those with?"

He looks at the retro design on the pink can of *Tab* and puts on a humorous expression. "There was already a good supply of it when I moved in, and it mixes up pretty nicely." He squeezes lime into the drinks, places a slice on the rim and gives them each a stir with the knife. He steps over, hands her a glass and they clink their glasses together.

She raises her eyebrows playfully and pronounces a toast. "To old friends…"

"They're the best to keep around."

They both take a sip, and Elizabeth moves over to sit on the couch. She puts her glass down on the coffee table and, perplexed, looks up at Jon. "What's this?"

Jon walks over, sits down beside her and places his cocktail next to a folded piece of paper with an antique gold coin placed on top. He picks up the treasure and examines it. "Looks like that coin Chaz found while diving in Jamaica." Jon exchanges a look with Elizabeth, hands her the coin, and unfolds the paper note. It reads:

Hey there, buddy, I just made it back stateside, but didn't have the time to stick around and say a proper Hello and Goodbye. Off on another deployment for the government and will be back in a few short months. Had to stash the skull in Jamaica to get off the island, but will retrieve it with you at our earliest convenience – Hey, just another adventure! Your pal, Chaz

Finished reading, Jon turns the note over to the blank backside. He drops it to the table, and his gaze searches around the apartment. Astounded, Elizabeth comments, "Does this mean he was just here?"

"I'm not too surprised… Somehow, he was able to get back before we did."

In the dim light of the apartment, she looks over the antique coin and offers it back to Jon. "Here… This is yours."

"No… We found it with your map."

Smiling, Elizabeth leans in closer and presses the gold coin into Jon's hand. "You take it." Her eyes dance gleefully, and her smile beams radiantly. "When you bring the map and the other treasure to California, I don't want any excuses about you not having the funds to visit me and stay awhile."

Holding the coin, Jon gazes into her bright, shining eyes. He wraps his arm around her shoulder and pulls her close. "I've got all the treasure I need right here."

With a flip of his hand, Jon tosses the coin to the coffee table. It spins for a short while, before it wobbles to a rest between the two unfinished cocktails.

The End…

If you enjoyed ***Conch Republic vol. II***,
read other stories by
Eric H. Heisner
www.leandogproductions.com

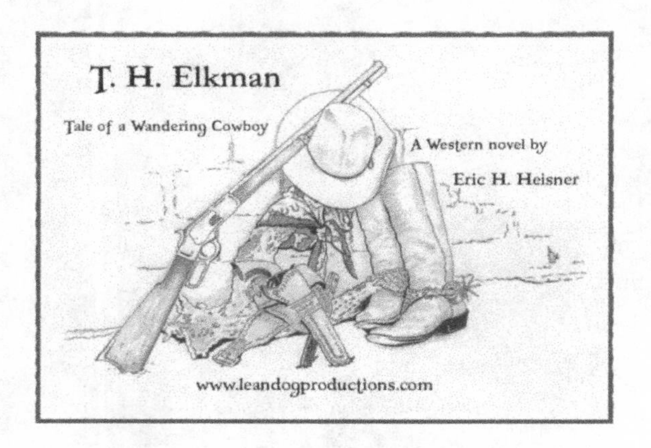
T. H. Elkman
Tale of a Wandering Cowboy
A Western novel by
Eric H. Heisner
www.leandogproductions.com

WEST TO BRAVO
A Western Novel
By Eric H. Heisner
WWW.LEANDOGPRODUCTIONS.COM

Wings of the Pirate
A high-flying Adventure Novel
By Eric H. Heisner
Limited time pre-order at:
www.inkshares.com
illustrations by
Al P. Bringas
www.leandogproductions.com

Eric H. Heisner is an award-winning writer, actor and filmmaker. He is the author of several Western and Adventure novels: *West to Bravo, T. H. Elkman, Africa Tusk, Conch Republic* and *Short Western Tales: Friend of the Devil.* He can be contacted at his website: www.leandogproductions.com

Emily Jean Mitchell is an artist, teacher, and mother who enjoys spending time in the garden and outdoor playtime with her husband, children and dog in Austin, Texas. www.mlemitchellart.com

HEMINGWAY'S"BOAT"
S.O. PILAR
KEY WEST, FL

A Very Special Thanks to:

Papa Richard Filip
- Hemingway Winner 2017 -

Printed in the USA
CPSIA information can be obtained
at www.ICGtesting.com
LVHW091917271023
762357LV00028B/207/J